CROSSTIES

BARBARA PURBAUGH

CROSSTIES

A NOVEL

Acknowledgements

WHEN I WAS ATTENDING GRADUATE SCHOOL GETTING MY CREATIVE WRITING degree, one of my professors said, "From the time you take your writing seriously to the time you publish, it will be twenty years."

Naturally, I was horrified. I had a lot of student loan debt, and I wanted to be on Oprah's Book Club List. But twenty years later, I realized that my professor was talking about the fact that writing is a craft that takes time to develop, so this book has been a twenty-year journey, but I'm glad it took me this long. If I had published my book twenty years ago, when I first thought it was complete, I would not be proud of it, and I am extremely proud of this book.

As you can imagine, if a book takes twenty years to write, it involves a lot of people who need to be acknowledged.

First and foremost, my family. The bad ones taught me who I didn't want to be, and the good ones made me who I am. A special thank you to my sister, Tammy, who is my best friend, and I'd be lost without her.

Next, Conrad, my benefactor, my cheerleader, and my friend, he never stopped believing in me or my dream. My friend, Bill, his support of my writing and me was invaluable.

To my writing friends, especially Janet and Sharon, who patiently read countless drafts of this book and never faltered in their belief that I would be a published writer someday.

I need to acknowledge my other friends. They see me in ways I never see myself and love me when I am least deserving of love.

I've been writing since I was 15, so there's a list of teachers that contributed to this book and to my education: F. Dale Baer, Kimberly McKenzie, Paul Daniel, Jr., Carol Shaulis, the entire English department at the University of Pittsburgh at Johnstown circa 1994-1998, (I'd list them all, but they know who they are and what they meant to me), and my professors at Naropa University, especially Bobbie Louise Hawkins, Keith Abbott, and Junior Burke.

I also must acknowledge all the therapists and counselors who got me through some rough patches in my life and made me mentally healthy enough to not only write this book but also finish it.

Thanks to Hannah Purbaugh for the cover design.

CHAPTER 1

We walked along the railroad tracks, and the heat from the rails scorched through my black tennis shoes, and my glasses kept sliding down my nose. My little sister, Joan, walked behind me on the wooden crossties. She had stopped balancing on the metal rails because it burned her feet through her Scooby-Doo flip-flops.

We had been swimming in the sulfur-soaked river, and it made our hair stiff and orange. Joan held a wet Barbie and Ken doll. Barbie wore a wedding dress, and Ken was naked. When we reached the last house along the tracks, we slid down over the bank into our backyard. Our dog barked furiously.

"Hush, Charlie dog," Joan said.

Charlie stopped barking and walked happily beside her.

We walked into the kitchen through the back door. There was a hole in the screen door taped with green masking tape. The kitchen smelled like fried potatoes and onions. My grandpa, wearing blue and pink plaid pants and a white undershirt covered with brown food stains, stood over the stove with a bent spatula in his hand, "Well, if it ain't the river rats," he said with a grin. He was missing some teeth, and when he smiled, he looked like a jack o' lantern.

The witch peeked out from the clock on the wall and chimed the noon hour.

"The witch is out," Joan said, pointing to the clock.

"Yep," Grandpa said as he flipped the potatoes over. "Sure to be bad weather soon."

If the boy and girl peered out of the clock, the weather was good. If it was the witch, bad weather was on its way. We watched as the witch slid back inside the clock. Grandpa placed the potatoes on our plates: my plate had yellow flowers and Joan's was white with red trim. We each got a glass of grape Kool-Aid. I liked cherry best, but grape was what we had because the food stamps hadn't come yet. We had to wait for the mailman because we were the last house on his route. As we ate the fried potatoes with ketchup, I stared at the cupboard across the room. I knew what was in it: half of a bag of sugar, two packs of grape Kool-Aid, three cans of green beans, a bag of flour, a box of oatmeal, a box of Cheerios, a can of peaches, and half of a box of macaroni.

In the refrigerator, there was some cheese, three sticks of butter, half of a gallon of milk, a jar of jelly, and a bottle of maple syrup that dripped down the inside of the refrigerator door. On the yellow kitchen table, there was a jar of peanut butter and half of a loaf of bread. There was nothing but ice cubes in the freezer.

I started figuring out how many meals we could make if the food stamps didn't come: oatmeal for breakfast, Cheerios for lunch, macaroni and cheese for supper, only I didn't know if we had enough cheese. Maybe we could eat the green beans for supper, but green beans didn't taste so good without something like ham.

I watched a group of flies gather on the bread bag, and I wondered why they weren't sticking to the yellow flypaper strips that hung from the ceiling as I shooed them away with my hand. I wondered what my mom and her new kids were eating. I saw them once at the grocery store. My mom's two babies have blonde hair like her. Joan and me have brown hair. I looked at Joan. Her hair was starting to dry, and it was stiff and matted like an old dog.

I wondered what my daddy was eating. Everyone at school said that the food in prison must be awful, and Mitchell Maxwell said that one time he was allowed to stay up late and watch a movie about prison, and he said that in prison, you get treated mean, and that if you are a man, they make you do stuff with other men. I knew no one could make my dad do anything he didn't want to do because he's big and mean.

My uncle, Jack, likes to talk about when my dad and him were sinners. Grandpa said it was bragging. Uncle Jack got religion now, and he preaches at the First Baptist Church on Wednesday nights. I wondered what Uncle Jack was eating. Grandpa said he lived high on the hog with all them church donations.

After we finished eating, we put our dishes into the sink. It was already full of dirty dishes.

"Suppose we'll do those tonight," Grandpa said, but we knew we wouldn't. There were still some clean dishes in the cupboard, and we never washed the dishes until we were drinking out of the jelly jars in the back. We wandered out onto the front porch to wait for the mailman.

I was expecting a letter from my dad. I had been writing to him for two years since my fourth-grade teacher, Mrs. Noble, helped me get the address. At first, I didn't tell Grandpa. I didn't know if he would like it, so I mailed the letters from school. But when my dad started writing back, I had to tell Grandpa. When the first letter came, Grandpa turned it over and over in his hand like something was going to pop out of it then he opened it and read the first three lines.

Helen,
I am glad you wrote to me. Long time since I heard from anyone in the family. I am glad that you like school…

Grandpa handed the letter back to me and muttered, "Some folks got to learn things on their own."

He never said anything more after that, and Dad wrote me every week. Mostly, he talked about things he read and told me funny stories about people in prison. I didn't think he was all that bad.

Once before she left, I asked my grandma about him. She was sitting on her bed reading her Bible when I asked her. Her face got all stiff and mean. "Your father is pure evil! If the Good Lord and me have anything to say about it, he's going to burn in the everlasting fires of hell!" She slapped the Bible hard. "It says so right here! And you are never to mention his name in this God-fearing house again! Understand?"

I understood. And I spent a lot of time thinking about my dad in prison and worrying if I was going to get sent there. Sometimes, I thought that my dad was the devil. Sometimes I thought he was Al Capone. I learned about Al Capone on TV, so I thought my dad must be like him.

Of course, I knew why he was in prison. I found out a couple of years ago when those blabbermouth Maxwell brothers felt the need to tell everyone in school.

"Theft and receiving stolen property," Mark Maxwell said, standing with his legs apart like he was the cop that had arrested him.

I remember everyone got real quiet, and I didn't say anything because I didn't really know what he'd done, but then when it was recess, Mrs. Noble told me it was true. That's when she helped me get my dad's address.

The clock in the kitchen struck one, and I looked through the window.

"The witch again," I said.

Grandpa looked at the sky. He rocked the porch swing, back and forth slowly like the pendulum we saw at the science museum in second grade.

Joan sat on the porch steps with her head in her hands. She was humming. Joan was always humming. Sometimes, she hummed songs we knew. Mostly, it was songs she made up. Charlie licked her toes, and she giggled. A group of ants had gathered an army and were marching steadily up the porch railing, and a breeze began to blow.

"Helen, what does your father write to you about?" Grandpa asked. The question hung in the air, heavy and suffocating. A train whistle blew in the distance, and we listened as the train rumbled nearer and nearer. Charlie ran to the backyard to bark at the train. When the train passed by our house, the house shook. I felt the vibrations along the porch railing, and the army of ants slid backward a little.

"Mostly, he writes about what he reads," I blurted out. The train echoed in the distance, and the vibrations stopped. Charlie returned and lay panting next to Joan.

"He didn't have no interest in readin' before."

"He says he likes it now. He says they've got a lot of books in prison."

I tried to match Grandpa's coolness but failed. I was scared. I wanted to defend my dad but couldn't because I didn't know how Grandpa felt about him. I knew Grandma hated him for sure, but I didn't know about Grandpa.

"Is that all he writes about?"

I watched the ants regroup and struggle up the rail.

"He tells funny stories about people in prison."

"I can't see as there's anything funny about prison."

Joan came to stand next to me. Her hair was completely dry now, and it stood up and out like strange feathers. I didn't know what to say to Grandpa. He stood up from the swing. "He tell you what he did?"

"I know," I said, suddenly taking an interest in one of the holes in my shoe.

"He tell you the whole story?" he asked.

I felt an ache in my stomach. What did he mean, the whole story?

"What's the whole story?" Joan blurted out. I took her hand. We stood so close together that the wind blew her stiff hair against my face.

Grandpa sighed, looked at the sky, then at the swing, which was swinging slower and slower.

"He'll have to tell you that someday. Maybe, someday, we'll all know."

The screen door squeaked as Grandpa opened it. He stood with his back to us. "I'm glad he's readin' now." He disappeared into the house.

Joan and I didn't move right away. We stood holding hands. Charlie wandered into the backyard; we heard him barking. I released Joan's hand, and she sat back down on the front stairs and began humming again. I reached out my hand to stop the swing.

Finally, the mailman's car came into view. It was a rusty maroon station wagon. We watched the car approach. Mr. Webb was the mailman's name. He was a large man with a beard who always smiled and waved as if he were really happy to see us. Joan and Charlie ran to greet him, and he gave Joan the mail and a handful of lollipops. It was 1976 and the Bicentennial, so all the lollipops were red, white, and blue. Grandpa stepped out onto the porch and waved. Mr. Webb waved back, turned the car around, and drove away.

Joan brought the mail to Grandpa. One envelope contained the food stamps. First thing tomorrow, we would go into town to the grocery store. I searched the envelopes for my dad's handwriting. It wasn't there, and he always wrote me once a week. Now, two weeks had passed, and I had heard nothing.

I sighed, and Grandpa looked at me. I went with Joan to spend the rest of the afternoon playing. Yesterday, Joan had given birth to triplets, and I had worked as her nanny and butler until I won an Oscar and became a movie star. Today, Joan would be a teacher, and I would be her student until I grew up and had triplets.

When Grandpa called us back inside for supper, we ate macaroni and cheese. While we ate, the witch came out of the clock and fell to the floor. Grandpa put her on the table and promised to glue her later.

Later, Joan took a bath in our old cast iron bathtub. She washed the sulfur out of her hair, making the water turn orange. After I took my bath, we changed into our nightgowns and combed our hair. Our hair was still wet, and it clung to our faces. Water dripped down her back as I combed the tangles out of Joan's hair. We ran outside to sit on the porch and watch the fireflies. We caught a few in a jar, but Grandpa made us release them. A truck was coming slowly down our road. We watched its headlights. Few cars traveled down our road and fewer still at night.

"It's Jack," Grandpa said as the truck halted in front of our house.

Uncle Jack got out of his truck. "Jackson Cooper Landscaping" was painted on the truck door. He wore a black suit with a tie the color of blood, red-brown. It was Wednesday, and he'd just come from the church. His face was flushed, and he talked rapidly. His glasses kept sliding down his nose.

"Dad, I got to talk to you," he shouted.

"What are you shouting about?"

"You know," Uncle Jack said.

Joan was lying on the porch swing, falling asleep. She raised her head to look at Uncle Jack.

"Well, come inside," Grandpa said, rising from the swing. I stood up. "Stay here," he commanded. I waited until Grandpa and Uncle Jack went into the kitchen, then I snuck into the dark backyard and listened through the screen door.

"How'd you find out?" Grandpa said.

"Mom," Uncle Jack said.

"That woman never could keep her mouth or her legs shut," Grandpa said.

"How long have you known?" Uncle Jack said.

"Lower your voice," Grandpa growled. "I've known since last week. He wrote Helen a letter."

"What are we going to do?" Uncle Jack asked.

"Not much we can do."

I leaned against the screen door. Why had Grandpa taken my letter? What did it say? I knew they were talking about my dad, and I knew Uncle Jack hated my dad, just as much as Grandma did, but Uncle Jack hated him for different reasons although I didn't know what his reasons were.

"You weren't going to tell me."

"I knew you'd get all bent out of shape like this."

A train whistle blew. The train rumbled closer and closer toward our house. By the time it passed and the screen door stopped shaking, Uncle Jack was in his truck driving away. I sat on the back step defeated because I hadn't heard the end of the conversation.

Later, after we had gone to bed, I couldn't sleep. I could hear the rain hitting the window. I could hear Grandpa breathing in the next room. Black lung had made his breathing labored and eerie.

Downstairs in the kitchen, I reached up and turned on the light by pulling the string, made of blue, green, and red yarn braided together, that hung over the kitchen table. The witch from the clock was lying on the table. I picked her up and held her in my fist. I wanted to glue her back into the clock, but I hadn't come downstairs to glue the witch. I had come looking for the letter. I searched through all the cabinets in the kitchen. In the last one, I found it, my dad's handwriting on the envelope. The envelope was addressed to me, but Grandpa had opened it. He hadn't done that since the first letter. I read my letter.

Helen,

You won't hear from me for a while. I'm getting out of prison. Don't know where I'll be. Don't think I'll come home. Don't know if I'd be welcome there. I will write again soon. I love you.

Dad

I folded the letter and put it back in the envelope. Why had Grandpa read this letter? Had someone told him that my dad was getting out of prison? Did he read the letter to be sure? Or did Grandpa know my dad was getting out of prison because he knew how many days my dad was gone? Did he miss him? Had Grandpa ever written to my dad? I had never seen a letter, but maybe Grandpa hid those letters, too. I quietly crept upstairs and back into bed. A train whistle blew, and the house rumbled. My dad was getting out of prison, and my stomach ached. My dad had never said he loved me before. I listened to Grandpa breathing in the dark.

CHAPTER 2

The sheriff sat in our living room on Grandma's gold chair with one leg bent and the other sticking straight out, right over the red stain in the carpet. Grandma had bought the carpet at a flea market. She paid twenty dollars for it; the stain came with it. Grandma said it was a wine stain, and she could get it out, but Grandpa said it was blood, and it was never coming out. Under the stain, the carpet was gold with blue flowers. The sheriff's boots were black and shining, and his arms were folded in front of him.

Grandpa sat on the edge of the couch looking like he was going to jump up and run away. He wore a white t-shirt and a pair of lime green pants. The t-shirt had a hole in the front of it, and the gray hair on his chest poked through it. Joan sat next to him. Her hair was pulled back into a tight, matted ponytail, and she had a purple Kool-Aid stain on her upper lip.

Charlie was on the front porch barking loudly.

"I don't think Charlie likes him," Joan whispered, but it was so quiet in the room we all heard her.

"That's because he doesn't know me," the sheriff said. He smiled without showing his teeth. His oily black hair was combed straight back.

I stood in the doorway wiping the lenses of my glasses on the hem of my t-shirt. There was a turtle on my shirt. Without my glasses, it was a green blur. When I put my glasses back on, the sheriff was struggling to get out of Grandma's chair because something was wrong with the leg that stuck straight out. His gun made a dull thud as it bounced against the arm of the chair.

"What's wrong with his leg?" Joan whispered to Grandpa.

"Old war wound," the sheriff said.

"You didn't get that in the war," Grandpa said, staring at the sheriff's leg.

"Now, George," the sheriff said. He was smiling again without showing his teeth. I wondered if he had any teeth. They were probably black or yellow or green. Charlie quit barking.

"Well now, Helen," the sheriff said, bending forward to look me in the eye. He smiled as he patted my head like a dog. He was missing some of his teeth, and the ones that were left were yellow.

He must have lost is teeth in the war, too, I thought, or someone knocked 'em out.

"Helen," the sheriff said, inching his large body closer to me with his hand still on my head. His breath was hot on my face; it smelled like onions. "I understand you have been getting letters from your dad." He said it like I'd done something wrong, and my stomach began to hurt.

"No," I said. It was the first lie I ever told, and it was a big one. I thought I was going to throw up on the sheriff's shiny black boots.

"Now, Helen," he said as his hand moved down to my shoulder. "Now, Helen, you know that isn't true. You know he's been writing to you, and I know it, too. You don't have to be afraid of me. I'm not going to hurt you."

"It is true," I said, adding to my lie. My stomach hurt more now.

The sheriff straightened his back and stopped leaning toward me, but his hand remained heavy on my shoulder. He started to squeeze my shoulder. "The law don't like liars," he said. "You know what the law does to liars."

I shook my head. His hand was squeezing harder and harder. My stomach hurt more and more.

"They put liars like your daddy in prison."

"My daddy didn't go to prison for lying," I said.

The sheriff laughed without showing his teeth. He stared at the top of my head, and his hand squeezed tighter until I cried out in pain.

Grandpa jumped up from the couch. "That is enough," he said. His eyes were open wide, and his hands shook.

The sheriff released my shoulder slowly and turned to look at Grandpa. I rubbed my shoulder.

"Calm down now, George," the sheriff said, talking to Grandpa like he was old. "You and I both know it's for the best. We need to know exactly what Sonny is up to."

"Suppose Samson ain't up to nothing. Suppose he's just comin' home." Grandpa was angry. His face was red, and he was breathing with rapid gasps.

"Now George, you know that ain't the best thing for him to do," the sheriff said.

"You mean it ain't the best for you." Grandpa shook and spit flew from his mouth as he talked. "Let's lay it on the table, Harvey. Girls," Grandpa was talking to us, but he was looking at the sheriff. "This man here is your mama's new husband."

Joan and I looked at each other.

"That's right. He's married to your mama, and he's worried that when your daddy comes back she'll be takin' up with him again. Ain't that right, Harvey?"

"I ain't worried about that," Harvey said, his face growing red. "She knows when she's got it good."

"Then what is it? What is it you're worried about? Maybe you'll get busted in the face again? Shot in the leg again?" Grandpa shook all over, and I could hear his watch rattling against the coins in his pocket. A train whistle blew.

"I ain't worried 'bout that. I just don't want any more of your sons to get killed." The sheriff's voice was so soft that I could barely hear it over the train that was shaking the house.

"You mean you don't want to kill them," Grandpa said. His voice was as soft as the sheriff's. I could hardly hear them over the roar of the train. It seemed to be coming through our house, shaking pictures and rattling the walls.

"That mountain was full of stolen car parts. They were breaking the law. I was just doing my job."

"State of Pennsylvania gave Samson five years. He served his time. Let him be." Grandpa looked at me. "Let them be. You got their mama, and she's got other kids. Let them be."

The train stopped behind our house, roaring and roaring. The floor vibrated, and I thought the house might explode. Charlie came running inside and hid under the sofa. A glass of purple Kool-Aid spilled onto the coffee table.

Then, the train was gone, and there was silence. Grandpa was breathing hard in short gasps. Joan sat on the couch; her feet dangled over the rug with the red stain. The sheriff put his hat on and turned around to leave.

The screen door squeaked open, and my dad stood there. I recognized him from a picture in Grandpa's wallet. He held a large gym bag. His hair was long, and his nose was bent. He wore a pair of dirty jeans and a neon yellow t-shirt.

He was so tall that his head reached the top of the doorway. He squinted to adjust to the change in the light.

"Am I welcome here?" he said to Grandpa.

Grandpa nodded. My dad dropped the bag, and it hit the floor with a thud.

"Did you come on the train?" Joan asked.

"Yes," he said softly. "I took the Greyhound into Somerset, but Lefty Ford still drives the train through here, so he was willing to give me a ride." He smiled at Grandpa.

"You're my dad," Joan said.

Dad looked at the sheriff for the first time. There was a look on his face that made me back up against the wall, and Joan slid back further on the couch.

"Yes, Joan, I am," he said.

Suddenly, Grandpa became unfrozen. "Come in, Samson. Don't just stand there."

My dad took one step forward. He never stopped looking at the sheriff. "Why are you here, Harvey?"

The sheriff cleared his throat and shifted his feet to stand with his legs apart. "People are worried about you coming back."

"People or you?"

"Now, Sonny, that ain't fair. I got a responsibility to the people of this town. We don't need any trouble like we had before."

"I ain't going to talk about that in front of my kids or ever again. That's in the past." It sounded like a warning.

The sheriff and my dad stared at each other.

"He's just worried about you taking up with Amy again," Grandpa said.

"She's your problem now," my dad said.

"Watch what you say," the sheriff said. His voice got loud, and his face was red.

"Relax, Harvey," my dad said, taking one more step into the living room, "Tell your people that I've been reformed." He rubbed his hand over his crooked nose.

Charlie began walking in and out of my dad's legs.

"Charlie likes you," Joan said.

"Charlie and me are old friends," he said, bending down to pet Charlie's head.

When he stood up again, the sheriff was standing close to him. "Remember, I'm watching you."

My dad smiled, showing a row of white teeth. "You've been watching too many cop shows, Harvey." He patted the sheriff's shoulder. The sheriff jumped back like my dad had burned him. He turned and walked out the door.

My dad reached into his shirt pocket and removed a pack of cigarettes. He slipped one into his mouth and followed the sheriff outside. He stood on the front porch and watched as the sheriff was getting into his car.

"Harvey," my dad shouted.

The sheriff stopped. He stood with one leg in the car and the other one out. My dad lit the cigarette and placed his hands on the porch railing. The railing was rotting, its green paint fading and peeling.

"Harvey, the past is in the past. Let's leave it there." He sucked on the cigarette and squinted against the sun.

The sheriff climbed into the car, slammed the door, and drove away. My dad squeezed the porch railing hard. The cigarette fell from his mouth, bounced against the railing, and landed in the yard. When he lifted his hands, I saw splinters in them.

I stood against the porch swing, and Joan stood in the doorway just a little behind Grandpa.

"Well, Helen," my dad said. I jumped. Joan slid further behind Grandpa. My dad turned around; he was grinning, and all his white teeth were showing. "It's good to see you again."

CHAPTER 3

Later in the grocery store, my dad pushed the grocery cart, and I watched his back. His neon yellow t-shirt glowed brightly. My grandpa walked beside him. I could see the food stamps sticking out of Grandpa's back pocket. I held the grocery list in my sweating hand and walked behind them.

The grocery list was written in orange crayon with Grandpa's scratchy handwriting. When my grandma wrote the list, it was always in black pen. Her handwriting was pretty with loops and curves.

I wondered where my dad got his neon-yellow t-shirt and how his jeans got so dirty and what it was like to ride on the train and how many days he'd been out of prison, but I still couldn't talk to him. I couldn't make the words come out. My throat was hot and dry, and my stomach felt like it was on fire.

The grocery store was filled with people, but it was quiet. There was no music coming from the speakers. None of the babies cried. No kids threw a fit. The only sound was Joan's hum. In the toilet paper aisle, Uncle Jack appeared. He wore a gray suit and a white tie. The lenses of his glasses turned yellow when he looked at my dad.

"Well, well, if it isn't the prodigal son," he hissed.

"Hello, Jackson," my dad smiled.

"What's wrong with you, Dad?" Uncle Jack said to Grandpa. "Why did you let him stay with you?"

"Where else was he gonna go? He's family."

"What about the girls? They're family. What happens when the welfare people come to take the girls away?"

I hugged my stomach, trying to make it stop hurting. Joan squeezed the toilet paper and kept humming.

"Relax, Dad," my dad said, patting Grandpa's arm. "That's not going to happen."

"Oh really, Mister Big Shot just out of prison, and how do you plan on preventing it?"

My dad looked at Uncle Jack's suit and grinned. "Still preaching on Wednesday night, Jackson?"

"Yes," Uncle Jack replied proudly.

Joan hummed louder. She squeezed the toilet paper and rocked back and forth.

"Stop humming," Uncle Jack growled. Joan looked stunned, dropped the toilet paper, and stepped back.

My dad stepped between Joan and Uncle Jack. He leaned forward to whisper in Uncle Jack's ear. "I like Joan's humming. It sounds good to me. Better than your hymns. Back off."

Uncle Jack stepped back. Joan picked up the toilet paper and moved to stand behind me.

"Maybe you need to hear some more hymns."

"Why? So, I can be like you? I don't think so." My dad leaned forward again and whispered in Uncle Jack's ear. "I know who you are, what you are."

"You don't know anything."

"I know, Jackson. I know."

My dad leaned back, reached into his pocket, and pulled out a cigarette. He lit it, rolled it between his fingers then took a puff from it. He watched Uncle Jack. Uncle Jack was so mad that he was shaking.

"Dad, don't you know what a fuss this is making around town?"

"The only one making a fuss is you." Grandpa stood with his hands on the grocery cart. He was trying to get Uncle Jack to calm down.

"How'd you know I was out?" my dad asked Uncle Jack.

"It's a small town. No one keeps secrets for long."

"I'd keep that in mind if I were you."

"Keep your voice down, and stop saying those things about me. It's a lie! It's a sin! And I won't have you saying such things."

Spit was flying from Uncle Jack's mouth, and his glasses with the yellow glowing lenses slid down his nose.

"Jackson," Grandpa said. "Jackson, now ain't no one judging anyone here. Ain't no sin. Just people. Who they are, what they do, and what happens to them. Let's not make a scene here."

The manager and the assistant manager of the grocery store stood at one end of the aisle, whispering and pointing. A group of people had gathered at the other end of the aisle. My dad looked at the manager and assistant manager, patted Grandpa on the arm, and said, "I'll wait in the car, Dad."

Grandpa nodded. We watched my dad's neon yellow t-shirt as he walked down the aisle.

Suddenly, Uncle Jack shouted, "No sins, Dad! No sins! What about the sin of killing your brother? What about that sin? What about the fact that he got Harrison killed?" Uncle Jack pointed at my dad's back. My dad's shoulders bent forward like he'd been hit. I swallowed hard.

This morning, Grandpa said the sheriff killed Uncle Harrison. I knew both my dad and Uncle Harrison went to Vietnam, so I figured that's how Uncle Harrison died, but now, I knew for sure someone had killed him. The sheriff said something about a mountain and stolen car parts. Is that what my dad stole? But what did Uncle Harrison have to do with that?

Joan stood next to me with the toilet paper still in her hands. I looked at her, and she looked at me.

"We made mistakes, and he died." My dad sounded like he was in pain.

"Okay, so it was a mistake! A mistake!" Uncle Jack looked at Grandpa. "Your son is dead because of him. My mother left you because of him, and it's a mistake!"

Joan dropped the toilet paper again.

I looked at Grandpa. His eyes were closed. I knew this day was coming. The day Grandpa would have to tell us the truth about Grandma. When we asked where she went, he had just said, "She's gone." Now, we would know the truth, but I wasn't so sure I wanted to hear it.

My dad kept walking, and I ran up the aisle after him. We passed the manager and assistant manager.

"We don't want any trouble in here," the manager said weakly.

We kept walking.

Outside, in the bright sunlight, the grocery baggers were huddled together and talking excitedly.

"Yeah, he's a big motherfucker. I saw him."

"Yeah, I thought he was going to punch his brother."

"Yeah, that queer preacher was really throwing a fit."

They spit tobacco onto the pavement. When they noticed my dad and me, they shut up.

Inside the car, my dad sat in the front seat, smoking his cigarettes, and I lay on the back seat holding my stomach.

No one said anything on the way home. Grandpa drove the car. It made a low growling sound. Joan still hugged the toilet paper. My dad smoked his cigarettes, throwing the butts out the window. I watched them sail out the window, their orange glow bouncing against the bubbling tar road. The inside of the car was hot, and I felt sweat drip down my back. My stomach hurt more and more. My dad reached over and turned on the radio. A loud, grinding song came from the speakers behind my head. My hand gripped the door handle. I leaned forward, and my glasses hit the floor. My dad muttered something that I couldn't understand.

Grandpa stopped the car at the edge of the road, and my dad lifted me out of the car. I puked on my dad's boots, but he didn't move just held me up. When I was done, he wiped my face with the end of his shirt. Grandpa got out of the car to check on me. He was sweating. Without my glasses, Grandpa was a blur. I still held onto the edge of my dad's shirt.

Grandpa and my dad looked at each other. Grandpa put my glasses back on, and we got back inside the car.

When we got home, Grandpa sat the grocery bags down onto the porch, stood up, and pointed down the railroad tracks. "Grandma lives about five miles down the tracks with Billy Jacobs."

Billy Jacobs was a gas station attendant in town. He drove a green Jeep, and he was 21. Joan and I looked at each other.

CHAPTER 4

IT WAS MORNING. WHEN I WALKED INTO THE LIVING ROOM WEARING MY NIGHT-gown, I saw my dad asleep on the floor over the red stain in the carpet. He had taken off his shirt and used it as a pillow. I didn't understand why he hadn't slept on the couch, but Uncle Jack was sitting there now. Billy Jacobs was crouched down in the corner under the window, and there, in her gold chair, sat my grandma. Her foot dangled just above my dad's sleeping head.

I hadn't seen her since I was nine. I remembered that she smelled like strong flowery perfume, and she always went to Bible studies and prayer meetings, and she hated my dad.

"Are you going to wake him?" Uncle Jack whispered to her.

There was a ray of sunlight shining into the room, and it made my dad's bare feet glow.

My grandma wore red high heels. She dropped her foot down onto my dad's head. My dad started, grabbed her ankle, and pulled her from the chair.

"What are you trying to do? Kill me?" Grandma screeched.

My dad released her ankle and sat up. "You shouldn't be kicking me."

Grandma struggled to her feet and looked down at my dad. The sunlight glowed around her head.

"Get up," she demanded.

My dad looked at her. He reached under the chair and pulled out a pack of cigarettes. He took one out, rolled it between his fingers, and lit it. The splinters from the porch railing were still stuck in his fingers, and I wondered if they hurt.

"Where's your worthless dad?" my grandma shouted at my dad.

Joan stood behind me. Her hair stood up on one side and was flat on the other. There was a rip in the arm of her nightgown, and she was chewing on her lower lip.

"Look at you," Grandma said, pointing at Joan, "You look like a bum. You never looked like that when I was around." She looked at Billy. "For years, I raised these kids, kids that weren't mine, and look at them now."

I looked at my grandma. She wore tight pants, and she had painted her lips and fingernails red. Her hair was dyed black and teased high. Had she always looked like that? I tried to remember but couldn't. Charlie came into the room and sniffed her legs.

"Get this mutt away from me." Charlie moved away from her to lie in the sun.

"Helen, where is your grandfather?" she demanded.

I shrugged, and she made a grunting noise.

I could tell Joan was excited to see her. I doubted she remembered much about her, but I think she thought she'd be like the grandmas on TV. She walked toward my grandma. I reached out my hand to try and stop her, but it was too late. She was standing in front of my grandmother. Before she could say anything, my grandma grabbed Joan by the arm and shook her.

"Where is your grandfather?" she said.

Joan started to cry. My dad stood up. There was a long ugly red scar across his chest, and he had a skull tattooed across his back.

"Don't ever touch my kid again," my dad said through clenched teeth. He pulled grandma's hand away from Joan's arm. "Joan, go to your grandfather," he said.

She ran crying from the room. Our grandma was nothing like the grandmas on TV.

Grandma laughed loudly. She stood on her toes trying to look my dad in the eye. "What are you going to do, Samson? What are you going to do? Kill me, too?"

"Mom, stop," Uncle Jack pleaded.

"Go ahead; I would welcome it," she said. "Every day, I was a good Christian woman. Every day, I prayed to God to strike you down. I was a good Christian woman. I took your children and tried to raise them to be good Christians, but they were filled with sin like you. But I raised them. I raised them because the

Lord and I had a deal. You would be smited for Harrison's death! And I would raise those children as good Christians. But the Lord, my God in heaven, that bastard cheated me! You're walking around a free man, and I know it was you; you killed Harrison! Now, God and I don't speak. 'Cause I don't pray. And I'm standing here a woman without faith 'cause the Lord took Harrison from me and left me with a murdering thief and a goddamn queer!"

Uncle Jack jumped up from the couch. "Mom! Mom! Don't say that! Those are lies. Mom, I am not a sinner. You got to stop saying things like that. Mom, you've got to stop saying that!"

"Shut up, Jackson!"

"Why are you here?" my dad asked, his voice low.

"To warn you that if God won't get you, I will." Grandma's voice was low and hard.

"What are you going to do, Mom?" my dad asked, smiling as he repeated her words.

Grandma stared at him. Her eyes were small and dark blue. One of her fake eyelashes had fallen, and it hung against her cheek like a spider.

"I'll take care of you. Don't you worry," she huffed. "Billy, let's go."

Billy Jacobs stood up from his position under the window. He didn't say anything, just followed Grandma out the door. We heard his Jeep start up and drive away.

The room was quiet. I watched Uncle Jack. He sat back down on the couch, shaking and breathing heavily. His blue tie moved with his breath. He slumped forward with his head in his hands. I sat in Grandma's chair. It smelled like her flower perfume, but the sunlight wasn't shining on it anymore.

My dad looked at Uncle Jack. He held a cigarette in his hand, and he rolled it back and forth between his fingers. Uncle Jack stood up. He was as tall as my dad but not as big.

"I didn't think she'd hurt Joan," Uncle Jack said.

"Have a cigarette," my dad said, tossing the pack at him.

"I stopped smoking," Uncle Jack said, not looking at my dad.

I wiggled in Grandma's chair. Uncle Jack put the cigarettes on the coffee table. The coffee table was painted sky blue, and someone's initials were carved in the side of it. I could read the letter "L" but nothing else. I didn't know where the coffee table came from. It was here before I was born.

"You still got your landscape business, Jack?" my dad asked. He stood against the wall, picking at the splinters in his hands.

"Yes." Uncle Jack seemed nervous like he wanted to run away.

"Doing okay?" my dad asked, picking up his neon yellow t-shirt from the floor and putting it on.

"Yes." Uncle Jack shifted from one foot to another like he had to pee.

Joan appeared in the living room. She wore a white dress, and her hair was pulled back into a crooked ponytail. You could tell she had been crying, but she was calm now. She walked over and sat in Grandma's chair next to me. I hugged her.

"How's Alex Coolie?" my dad asked. He leaned back against the wall with his head resting against a picture of Roy Rogers.

Uncle Jack sucked in his stomach like my dad had hit him.

My dad watched his reaction. "You don't see him anymore, do you?"

Uncle Jack shook his head.

"That's a damn shame. Alex was a good guy. For a little guy, he could fight. He was tough like his old man. Old Man Coolie still alive?"

Uncle Jack nodded.

"Damn, he must be a hundred years old." My dad laughed. "I bet he knows everything about everyone in this town."

Uncle Jack didn't say anything because he was too busy shifting his feet and trying to get something off his tie, but I didn't see anything on his tie. Joan moved from the chair to sit on the floor.

"Shit, Jack," my dad said, crushing his cigarette out into an ashtray that looked like a toilet. "Are you still pissed about that? Goddamn it. I was trying to keep you out of Vietnam. It was hell. Harrison was a dumb ass and enlisted. I couldn't stop him. You know no one could ever stop him from being stupid. But I could keep you from being drafted." My dad ran his hand through his hair, pushing it away from his face.

"My bad eyesight would have kept me from being drafted," Uncle Jack said. "You didn't have to say anything about the other thing. It could have stayed a secret."

"Jack, you can't take a piss in this town without people knowing about it. And I did it because I knew damn sure they wouldn't draft you if they knew," he paused, "about the other thing."

"You don't know what hell that caused me," Uncle Jack said.

"No but I knew Vietnam." My dad lit another cigarette. "I'm sorry for all the shit you had to take here. Really, I am. Hell, I don't know, Jack, maybe I did the wrong thing, but I thought it was right at the time."

"It doesn't matter," Uncle Jack said quietly. "I've changed. I ain't like that anymore."

There was a long silence. I watched Uncle Jack, his hand on his tie. The sun was shining on his head. He was going bald. I didn't think Uncle Jack looked much like my dad. My dad watched Uncle Jack as he stared at the floor. I could hear Charlie barking and the whistle of the train. Joan played with the hem of her white dress. I ran my foot across the red stain in the carpet, watching patterns form and reform. The house began to vibrate. I could feel the vibration of the train under my foot.

The picture of Roy Rogers began to bounce against my dad's head. My dad stepped forward, and Roy fell to the floor. The glass broke. The train moved on, and I walked into the kitchen to get a broom.

When I looked out the kitchen window, I saw Grandpa on the railroad tracks picking up Charlie. He'd been hit by the train. I knew Charlie was dead because there was blood on Grandpa's yellow pants. Behind me, I heard Joan scream, and I watched as she ran outside.

Uncle Jack and my dad walked past me and went outside. I went into the living room and swept up the broken glass. When I walked back into the kitchen, I put the picture of Roy Rogers on the kitchen table.

From the kitchen window, I watched as Grandpa brought Charlie down from the railroad tracks and handed him to my dad. Uncle Jack walked into the woodshed. When Joan started to cry, Grandpa bent down and talked to her, but I couldn't hear what he was saying.

I knew I should be upset about Charlie, but right now, I was thinking about my dad and the sheriff and Uncle Jack and our grandma.

Uncle Jack came out of the woodshed with two shovels. My dad took off his yellow shirt and wrapped Charlie in it. Grandpa stood next to Joan, holding onto her hand while Uncle Jack and my dad dug a hole next to the woodshed. When they were finished digging the hole, my dad lifted Charlie, still wrapped in the t-shirt, and put him into the hole. Joan hugged Grandpa as she cried. My dad and Uncle Jack covered Charlie with dirt, and I watched as everyone bowed their heads. I knew they were praying, but I didn't bow my head. My stomach hurt.

Grandpa and Joan walked back into the house, and Uncle Jack and my dad carried the shovels back into the shed, then stood in the doorway. They were talking, but I couldn't hear what they were saying. I heard Grandpa's car start, and I knew he was taking Joan somewhere. I ran to the front porch and watched as they drove away.

I heard Uncle Jack and my dad talking as they walked into the house. I watched them walk upstairs, and I heard the bathroom light snap on. The light in the bathroom hung over the toilet; they had to pull a string to turn it on. A bracelet hung from the string.

The bathroom was really small. When I sat on the toilet, I could put my hands in the sink. I wondered how Uncle Jack and my dad could both fit in the bathroom at the same time, and I wondered what they were doing in there. I wondered if they were talking about the thing that my dad had done. I suspected it had something to do with everyone calling Uncle Jack a queer. I wasn't sure what that was, but I'm pretty sure it wasn't a good thing.

I walked upstairs into Joan and my bedroom. I went to the dresser, pulled out a pair of jean shorts, and slid them on. I took my nightgown off and put on a yellow t-shirt. I combed my hair into a ponytail and used a red rubber band to hold it in place. After I put on my Scooby-Doo flip-flops, I walked down the hall toward the bathroom.

The bathroom walls were covered with purple-striped wallpaper that peeled in the corners. Over the sink, there were stickers that we had gotten in school: "Great Smile." "Brush your teeth." "Keep smiling."

The bathroom door was open, and I peered inside. My dad sat on the toilet with his hands in the sink. Uncle Jack stood over him, taking the splinters out of his hands with a small pocketknife. My dad didn't move, and he didn't seem afraid. He smiled as he talked to Uncle Jack. I stood in the doorway and listened.

"Damn, you must have a thousand in here," Uncle Jack said.

My dad laughed.

"This reminds me of that time that you and Alex and Harrison got into that fight over in Rockwood. You had so much glass in your faces, hands, and arms. It took me forever to get it out. I had to use mom's eyebrow tweezers," Uncle Jack said.

"And a ton of iodine. It burned like hell."

"Harrison cursed me for weeks."

"Yeah, that's why I ask you, Jack. I figured you were an expert."

"Was it bad?"

"The iodine? Hell no, not as bad as Harrison made it out to be."

"Not the iodine. Prison."

"Let's not talk about that, Jackson."

They were silent as Uncle Jack continued removing the splinters.

My dad noticed me standing in the doorway and smiled.

"Hi, Helen," he said. "Sorry about Charlie. It happens when you live close to the tracks. Are you okay?"

I nodded.

Uncle Jack was looking at me with a strange look on his face. He was smiling, and I took a step back.

I turned and ran down the stairs. I didn't know what to do once I was in the living room. Joan wasn't here. I stared at Grandma's chair, and it made me mad. I walked over and began pushing the chair toward the door. It took me awhile, but I pushed it out the front door and off the porch. It lay on its side in the front yard.

"I'll get Grandpa to burn it," I said. I ran back inside and grabbed the ugly, red-stained rug, and I tossed it on top of the chair. I sat down on the porch steps, proud of myself.

I could hear Grandpa's car coming. The growling noise had turned into a loud squeaking noise. My dad and Uncle Jack came outside. Uncle Jack had taken off his tie. My dad still wasn't wearing a shirt or shoes, and a cigarette dangled from his lips. He sat on the swing. Uncle Jack sat on the porch steps next to me. He had a cigarette in his hand.

"What are you going to do with those?" Uncle Jack asked, pointing at Grandma's chair and the rug.

"Burn them," I said.

"Good idea," my dad said, tossing his cigarette at the chair. It bounced off the chair and landed in the yard next to me. I stood up and crushed it with my flip-flop.

Grandpa's car pulled into the yard. The sheriff's car pulled in behind him. My dad stood up, and Uncle Jack sucked his cigarette loudly. Grandpa and Joan got out of the car. Her face was covered with chocolate ice cream, and she carried a box of Popsicles.

"I got you Popsicles," she said, hugging them tightly against her dress and carrying them inside. I sat down on the porch steps next to Uncle Jack.

"Don't get worked up, Samson," Grandpa whispered as he stepped onto the porch.

The sheriff climbed out of his car. Joe Williams was with him. Joe was a deputy who wore thick glasses and looked like a stick man with a big head and a skinny body.

The sheriff walked toward the house. His oily black hair dripped with sweat, and he smiled again without showing his teeth. He put his hands together and cracked all of his knuckles. Joe Williams held onto his gun tightly. His eyes were big under his glasses, and they moved back and forth from my dad to my Uncle Jack to my Grandpa and back again.

"Well, hello everyone," the sheriff said. He rested his bad leg on the bottom step.

No one or nothing moved except Joe's eyes.

"Sure is hot," the sheriff said. He pulled a notebook from the pocket below his silver star. "I got some reports of you, George, being seen at Floyd's Grocery Store with blood on your clothes. Figured I better check it out."

"Our dog got hit by the train. It's his blood. Joan was upset, so I took her for ice cream," Grandpa said.

"Um," the sheriff said, writing in his notebook. "That so. Well, that's too bad." The sheriff looked up at my dad. "About the dog. I mean." He smiled without showing his teeth.

My dad leaned forward and squeezed the porch railing.

"Well, I have to make sure nothing's wrong. You know with an ex-convict on the premises you've got to keep an eye out," the sheriff said, putting the notebook in his pocket.

My dad squeezed the railing, and the wood cracked. Pieces of wood flew into mine and Uncle Jack's hair. Joe jumped back and pulled out his gun.

The sheriff grinned, showing all the yellow teeth left in his mouth.

"Put the gun away, Joe, before you hurt someone or yourself," the sheriff said. "So, Sonny, I see you haven't lost your ability to fight. That's good." The sheriff looked at me. "Sorry about your dog."

Joe and the sheriff got into their car and drove away with the lights flashing and the siren blaring. My dad lifted his hands from the railing. I could see all the splinters in his hands.

"Jack, I think I'll need your help again."

Uncle Jack nodded. An unlit cigarette hung from his lips. Grandpa patted my dad's arm.

CHAPTER 5

Everything in the house smelled like the green beans and ham that Grandpa was cooking on the stove. He sat in the living room watching a bowling show on TV. My dad and Uncle Jack had gone somewhere in Uncle Jack's truck. I found Joan sitting on the floor of our bedroom with my dad's bag open in front of her.

"What are you doing?"

"Lookin'," she said, holding up a stack of letters wrapped with a string. The letters were the ones I wrote to my dad. Joan had taken things out of the bag; clothes, books, and photographs lay on the floor.

"It's us," Joan said, showing me a picture of us when we were smaller.

She held up another picture. "Look, it's Mom," she said. She handed the picture to me. My mom wore a purple dress, and her long blond hair was in a braid that lay on her shoulders. She leaned against a car. Uncle Harrison stood next to her. I recognized him from the pictures on the living room wall. Uncle Jack and a guy with a beard were in the background. Uncle Jack had his arm around the guy.

"Who's that?" Joan asked about the guy.

I shrugged.

I put the picture in my back pocket. "You better put this stuff away before he gets back," I said to Joan. I walked out of the bedroom. Downstairs, I ate a bowl of ham and green beans and a banana Popsicle. I put on my black tennis shoes.

"Where you going?" Grandpa asked.

"Outside for a while," I said as I walked out the back door. When I thought no one was looking, I walked past the woodshed. I was careful not to step on Charlie's grave as I headed down the railroad tracks.

Mr. Coolie lived about a mile away from us. We had to pass his house to go swimming. Sometimes, he was outside. He was a short, old man with a long white beard but no hair on his head. He didn't have any teeth either. Sometimes, he was outside in his underwear, the kind that looked like shorts. He grew lots of flowers and plants. His small house had no upstairs. From the railroad tracks, I could see that he had a window in his roof.

It was too hot to walk on the metal part of the railroad tracks today, so I hopped from one wooden crosstie to another. I took the picture out of my pocket. My mom was smiling, but Uncle Harrison wasn't. I put the picture back in my pocket.

When I got to Mr. Coolie's house, I was hot and tired. My glasses kept sliding down my nose, and my face was warm. I stood on the tracks and looked down at Mr. Coolie's house. My dad said he knew everything about everyone, and I hoped that included everyone in the picture. A big gray cat sat on a broken lawn chair in the yard. Mr. Coolie was in the yard in his underwear. His underwear had little red hearts on them. He sat on a tree stump, whistling. He was planting flowers in little green pots. He looked up and waved.

"Well, if it ain't the river rat from down the tracks." He smiled, and his gums shone pink in the sun.

I folded my arms against my chest.

"Goin' swimming?" he asked.

I didn't say anything. The gray cat jumped off the lawn chair, and the chair fell over. Mr. Coolie stood up and walked toward me. "You ain't got no sister or swimming gear. You here on business?"

"I got to ask you something," I said. My stomach hurt, and I was scared.

"Well, come on down off the railroad tracks before you get killed and ask me."

I walked down the bank. It was filled with flowers of different colors and sizes. I stood in Mr. Coolie's yard, and the cat sniffed me.

"Well, Helen," Mr. Coolie said, sitting down in the broken lawn chair. "Have a seat." He pointed to a green stool. I sat down on it. It was hot from the sun.

"Well, what do you want to know?" he asked. His hands planted tiny flowers in the black dirt. I took the picture out and showed it to him. He smiled. "That's my son, Alex," he said, pointing to the man with the beard. "He's an accountant in Johnstown. He and your Uncle Jack used to be real close." He pointed to Uncle Jack in the picture. "Then Jack went on his religious kick." Mr. Coolie rolled his eyes and sighed. "It broke Alex's heart. Alex is seeing a nice boy now. His name's Luke or Leo or something."

"So, my Uncle Jack likes other men?" I blurted out before I could stop myself. "That's what queer means?"

Mr. Coolie nodded. "Yeah but queer ain't a nice word." He looked at me. "And don't go believing all that going to hell and sinning stuff they'll tell you. Ain't no finer man than my son, Alex, and your Uncle Jack is a good man, too."

I must have looked doubtful.

"Now, your Uncle Jack had a hard time of it there for a while. Folks messed up his head; if he gets it right again, you'll see. You'll see how good he is."

"What about my mom?" I said, pointing at the picture.

Mr. Coolie shook his head and continued planting the tiny plants.

"Where does she live?" My stomach hurt, and I was afraid he wouldn't tell me.

He looked surprised then sad. "Your dad coming back isn't easy, is it?"

I didn't say anything. I was surprised that he knew that my dad was back, but then my dad said you can't take a piss in this town without everyone knowing it.

He stopped planting the flowers and looked up at me. "You're like your dad, tough as nails."

I put the picture back in my pocket.

"Why do you want to know?" he asked.

"Gotta ask her some things."

"What things?"

I looked at him. He looked at me, his wrinkled face frowning.

"Why she didn't want us anymore," I said it out loud. I didn't even know that was what I wanted to find out, and I was scared.

"What if she don't tell you or worse yet tells you something you don't want to hear?"

"I got to know."

The gray cat sat on my feet. Me and Mr. Coolie looked at each other. A train whistle blew, and a train rumbled toward us. We stared at each other. The ground began to shake beneath my feet. The hot wind from the train blew

Mr. Coolie's beard. The green stool shook under me. Mr. Coolie seemed to be deciding something as the lawn chair swayed under him. The train passed, and the lawn chair stopped swaying. Mr. Coolie smoothed his beard.

"If you go down the tracks about a mile past your swimming hole, there's a sign that says Wolfgang Street. There's a white house at the end of the street. Her and the sheriff live there."

I stood up. I didn't know if my knees were shaking because of the train or because he had told me.

"Be careful," Mr. Coolie muttered as he stood up and began to gather the tiny plants in his arms.

I climbed back up the bank of flowers and onto the railroad tracks.

"Be careful on those railroad tracks," Mr. Coolie shouted. His back was to me. "I had a daughter that got killed on them." He put the plants in rows along the side of his house, and then he looked at me. "Sorry about your dog."

I was surprised that he knew about Charlie.

"I got a telephone and a whole group of lady friends." He winked and grinned his toothless grin. "Besides, you can't take a piss in this town without everyone knowing it."

I headed down the tracks toward my mom's house. The sun was hot, and a few times I had to get off the tracks to let a train pass. I stood in the bushes until the train passed, and I got cuts on my legs. I had to get to my mom's house before it was dark, or the sheriff came home.

When I got to Wolfgang Street, my feet hurt, and I wanted to go home, but I had come this far, and I needed to know. When I reached my mom's house, I stood behind a tree at the end of the yard. The sheriff's car was not in the driveway. My mom had a big white house. The lawn was bright green, and there were no tire marks in it. I could see a plastic swimming pool that looked like a turtle and a swing set in the yard. Mom's kids were babies with blond hair and fat legs and faces. No one was in the yard, so I had to go to the door. I was scared, and my stomach was hurting more than my feet.

I walked across my mom's pretty green yard, up the sidewalk, and stopped at the front door. My mom had a screen door, and I could see into her house. Her furniture was new and the same color. There was no stain on her rug, and everything smelled like pine cleaning stuff. A fan whirled over the couch, and a game show played on a big colored TV.

My mom sat on the end of the couch folding clothes. Her long, blond hair was in a ponytail. My hands shook as I rang the doorbell. My mom turned around, stood up, and came toward the door. She smiled until she recognized me. The smile left her face as she whispered my name. She looked around as if someone might see us.

"What are you doing here?" she whispered. She looked outside over my head. "Who brought you here?"

"I came by myself down the railroad tracks," I said. Her eyes were blue. She wore a pair of white shorts and a red shirt.

"Why are you here?" She opened the screen door and stepped outside. I had to step back to let her out. She smelled like laundry detergent and cleaning stuff. "Does your grandpa know you're here?"

I shook my head. My mom wasn't very tall, just a little taller than me.

"You shouldn't be here," she whispered. "Did your dad send you?"

I shook my head, and she looked disappointed.

"I gotta ask you some things."

Her fingernails were bright blue. She began to chew on them. "You look like your daddy," she said "You've got his ways, too. The way you carry your-self. It's a lot like him." She reached out to touch my hair, and I stepped back.

"Why did you leave us?"

She started to cry with tears rolling down her face. "It was so hard. Your grandma could be so tough, and your dad was going to jail." The words were coming out in gasps. Grandpa liked to watch soap operas, and the women always cried like this. When they cried like this, they were lying.

"You're lying."

She stopped crying. "What did you say?"

The people on the game show were shouting. In the distance, I could hear a train. My mom's house did not shake.

"I asked you why you left us."

"And, I told you why." Her voice was low and angry. "What did you come here for? To cause trouble? You shouldn't be here."

My mother stepped toward me, and I backed away. The sheriff pulled into the driveway, and the lights of his car flashed across my mom's face.

One of the babies started to cry. As the sheriff opened the car door, the look on my mom's face changed. She didn't look angry anymore. She was smiling. I curled my hand into a fist. I could hear the baby crying louder, and I heard the music of the game show ending. The sheriff put his bad leg out of the car, and my mom kept smiling at him. The sun glistened off what was left of her fingernails. My stomach hurt. The crying baby appeared at the door with its face red and wet. "Oh now," my mom said to the crying baby. "Hush now, baby." She ran her hand over the baby's blond curls.

I pulled my fist back and punched my mom in the mouth. She screamed as blood gushed from her lip. I panicked and started running. I heard the sheriff's voice behind me. I ran back onto the railroad tracks. I could hear my tennis shoes hit the gravel, feel my heart racing.

When I reached the swimming hole, I was sweating and gasping for breath. I sat down by the river to catch my breath. It was getting dark, and I was scared. I knew I couldn't go home. I was a criminal now. I would be sent away for sure. I was too young for jail, but I knew the welfare people would come and take me away for sure. I lay down by the river. My hand hurt. I felt scared, tired, angry, and good all at the same time. My stomach didn't hurt anymore. I felt big and mean. I wondered if my dad felt this way.

I waited until it was dark to go home. I snuck behind the house and listened through the screen door.

I could hear the sheriff's angry voice. "She hit her in mouth. Look at her lip."

I knew this meant my mom had a swollen lip, and I felt good about it. I felt big and mean. I also knew that this meant my mom was in our house. If so, where were the fat babies? Where was Joan? Had she expected her to be a TV mom? Had she gotten hurt again?

"Is this how she's going to behave now that he's back in town?" the sheriff said.

No one answered him.

"I could arrest her, you know. I could call Child Protective Services."

There was still no answer.

"Well, you keep her away from my family. You hear?"

"There won't be any more trouble, Harvey," Uncle Jack said.

"Better not be," he growled. "Come on."

I listened as they left the house and drove away.

"Well, someone ought to be looking for her," Grandpa said. "She ain't ever been out alone after dark, and we don't want her on the tracks in the dark."

"Why'd she go there?" Uncle Jack asked. "I didn't know that she knew where they lived."

"Me neither."

"Well, we got to find her. Set her straight on how she can't be over there," Uncle Jack said.

I heard a rustling sound behind me. For a second, I expected Charlie, but I knew it couldn't be him. When I turned to see who it was, it was my dad coming off the railroad tracks with a flashlight in his hand. Had he been looking for me or hiding from the sheriff? Or both?

My dad approached me. I couldn't see his face clearly, so I didn't know if he was mad or not.

"Hear you been out causing trouble."

I opened my mouth to defend myself.

He shook his head. "No need to explain it. I know why. But you better come on inside. Your grandpa's worried, and Uncle Jack needs to give you a lecture." He smiled slightly. "Folks are right when they say you're a lot like me." He patted my head. "Better watch yourself. That feeling big and mean will get you in a lot of trouble."

I looked at him. How did he know I felt that way? Because he felt that way, I thought.

He opened the screen door, and we walked inside.

CHAPTER 6

The next day, my dad was moving things out of a small room upstairs. We used the room as a closet to hold our Christmas decorations. I stood in the doorway and watched him as he moved a large box filled with rocks, and when he did, several little black spiders scurried away.

"What are you doing?" Joan asked, peering into the room. She sucked loudly on a red Popsicle.

"Making a place for me to sleep," my dad said. He moved another box.

"You're going to sleep in here?"

"I'm planning on it."

"What are we going to do with our Christmas tree?"

The artificial Christmas tree leaned against the wall in its torn, dirty box.

"I'm sure we'll find a place for it. This thing must be twenty years old." He lifted the box and branches slid out of the bottom. "We had a tree like this in prison. Ugly."

Joan walked away.

"Here, Helen," my dad said handing me a box of old religious magazines. "Take these to the woodshed." The box was heavy, but I didn't say anything. I was tough, and I could handle it. The box hit the shed floor with a loud thump.

Upstairs again, my dad handed me a box of Christmas ornaments. They were covered with dust, and my hands turned gray then black. "Put those with the Christmas tree."

Joan appeared in the doorway to watch, but my dad didn't make her carry anything. My dad handed me a box of rocks.

"What are those?" Joan asked.

"Your Uncle Harrison collected rocks. There are about three more boxes in here."

I sat the box on the floor, and Joan opened it. It was filled with multi-colored rocks. We looked through the box, running our hands over every rock. My dad grunted and pulled on a box that was stuck in the corner. The box broke apart, and rocks came tumbling out and landed on his feet.

"Damn," he cursed.

Joan picked up all the rocks at my dad's feet. She was excited. "Can I keep them?" she asked.

My dad seemed surprised. "Well, I suppose. If you clean them up and get rid of the spiders, I don't see why not."

Joan jumped up and down. "Thank you, Daddy." She hugged him then ran with a handful of rocks into the bathroom. I could hear the rocks clang in the bathtub as she ran water over them.

I couldn't move. Joan had called my dad "daddy" like he'd always been here. She had hugged him like the girls on TV hugged their dads. Hadn't she learned anything from meeting grandma?

Last night, after Uncle Jack gave me a lecture and I promised not to go to my mom's house, I asked Joan what happened. Had she seen our mom and the sheriff? She said Grandpa made her go to our room, but she did try and listen at the top of the stairs, but all she heard was the sheriff being mad. Our dad was out looking for me, and she never got to see our mom. I was glad about that, but I knew Joan was disappointed.

My dad smiled as he went back to cleaning the room. I wasn't like Joan. I knew I'd never call him Daddy.

"Helen, go downstairs and get the bug spray."

When I sprayed the spiders, they ran crazy in every direction. My dad moved boxes of old clothes and toys from the room. There was a window in the room. I had never seen it before. My dad pulled a torn green blind from the window, and the room lit up. I looked out the window. You could see the front porch roof and down into the front yard.

A box fell from a shelf and hit my dad on the head. He cursed as photographs fell everywhere. My dad shook the dust from his hair and laughed. "Thank God, it wasn't another box of rocks."

I helped him pick up the photographs. They were of people I didn't know, weddings I hadn't been to. I remembered that I hadn't even asked Mr. Coolie about Uncle Harrison when I showed him the picture of my mom. I started to look through the pictures when my dad said, "Helen, take the last box of rocks to Joan."

I took the rocks to her. She had rows of clean, shiny rocks on the floor and on the windowsill. "Aren't they beautiful?" she said, smiling.

I had to admit they were

"I'll give you one. Which one do you want?"

I took a small blue one and put it in my pocket.

When I went back to my dad, all the pictures were gone.

All morning, my dad and I worked to clean the room. We used the whole can of bug spray on the spiders. The spiders left red bite marks on our arms and legs. We scrubbed the room with bleach water, but the spiders survived. My dad and I sat on the floor defeated.

"The spiders are winning, Helen," he said.

"We need different bug spray," I said. I pointed at the can. There was a picture of ants, not spiders on it.

We decided to go into town for the right bug spray. We walked into Maxwell's Hardware Store covered with dirt, dust, sweat, and spider bites. I followed my dad through the store. Everyone stared at us: Mr. Bailey and the other old men who always sat on a bench by the counter and Mrs. Applegate who was getting a set of car keys made. There was a lot of whispering and the rattle of nails at the back of the store.

The Maxwell brothers stood against the back wall. When school started, they would be in the sixth grade, too, but I was a lot taller than them. They hadn't had a growth spurt yet. At least, that's what their mother always said.

"Hey, Helen," Mitchell said.

"You boys quit clowning around back there and come up here," Mrs. Maxwell said from some unseen place.

"What you doing?" Mark said to me.

"Helping my dad," I said.

My dad was in the next aisle reading the labels on the bug spray cans.

"I heard he got outta prison. What's he like? Is he mean to you?"

"Nah," I said. I wanted to brag about my dad. Tell them what a great dad he was. How he fixed things around the house, read stories, and was just like the dads on TV. No, better than the dads on TV, but the best I could say was, "He's really nice."

This seemed to disappoint them, and they walked away to be with their mother.

"Come on, Helen," my dad said. "I got the bug spray."

I followed my dad to the counter. Mr. Maxwell rang up the bug spray, and my dad counted out his money. I knew it was all the money he had.

Mr. Maxwell seemed to know this, too. He smiled at me. "Helen, why don't you get a piece of candy for you and your sister?"

Maxwell's had a candy counter at the front of the store filled with tootsie rolls and fireballs.

I looked at my dad. His face was pulled tight, and I knew he was embarrassed because he didn't have enough money to buy those dumb old pieces of stale candy.

"No, thank you," I said politely.

Mr. Maxwell shrugged, and the boys giggled. They were standing behind the counter. I promised myself that the Maxwell boys would pay. Even if they had a growth spurt, I could still beat them. I was meaner now.

CHAPTER 7

Joan and I pretended we were Charlie's Angels on a secret mission as we walked to the swimming hole. I walked on the metal part of the railroad tracks without shoes. It burned my feet, but I didn't jump off right away. We hid in the weeds by Mr. Coolie's house to spy on him, but he wasn't home. His gray cat followed us down the tracks for a while then went home.

When a train came, we jumped off the railroad tracks and stood in the weeds. We waved to the man inside the train. He had a mustache that curled at the ends. When we were back on the tracks, Joan pretended that she was from France. I was from Ireland. We planned to overthrow the evil empress who lived in Texas. When we got to the swimming hole, we lay on our bellies and pretended to be watching the empress' house.

"What does her house look like?" Joan asked in her fake French accent.

"It's white and has matching furniture," I whispered back in my Irish voice. I watched a TV show about some leprechauns once, so I knew how to sound Irish.

"Is it pretty?"

"Guess so."

We inched along the ground, hoping to see the empress.

"What does she look like?" Joan whispered.

"Short, blond, wears ugly nail polish."

Joan hid behind the tree, hoping the empress wouldn't see her.

"I don't think she's here," Joan whispered.

"She must be at her summer home," I whispered back.

"What's it like there?"

"Smells like pine trees," I said, crawling backward away from the river.

Joan dropped down beside me and inched backward, too.

"Are we going there?"

Joan and I looked at each other.

"Do you want to?"

"What happens if the empress is there?"

I stood up. "I am trained in hand-to-hand combat." I cracked my knuckles loudly.

Joan stood up and whispered, "What if the sheriff is there?"

"No guard of the evil empress can stop me." I marched onto the railroad tracks, and Joan followed me. She began singing in her French voice, "No evil empress will stop us. No guard of the empress can stop us." We walked down the tracks and got off at Wolfgang Street.

When we got to my mom's house, we stood in the driveway and watched her babies playing in their turtle swimming pool. Their fat legs flew in the air when they slid down the sliding board. My mom sat at the picnic table looking at a magazine. The sun reflected off the bright pictures of models on the cover. My mom's hair hung down around her face in little blond curls. There were several bottles of nail polish in different colors sitting on the picnic table.

"The empress is here," I whispered.

Joan stepped into the grass, and there was no pretending anymore. I stayed in the driveway and watched Joan. Her Scooby-Doo flip-flops made a snapping sound as she walked across the yard. The babies stopped playing and watched her. My mom looked up. The magazine slipped from her hands. She didn't say Joan's name; she just stared at her. Joan sat down on the bench across from her.

"How did you get here?" my mom asked.

"Helen brought me," Joan said, turning to point at me.

My mom looked at me, and I looked back at her. My mom stood up, and the bottles of fingernail polish fell over. Joan carefully picked up each one and placed them in a row.

"I don't think you should be here," my mom said, looking at me. "You were warned to stay away."

"I wanted to see you," Joan said.

My mom looked like she wanted to run away. I stood in the driveway with my feet apart, and my arms folded. The driveway was hot, and I still wasn't wearing my tennis shoes, so my feet began to burn.

"Does your Grandpa know you're here?" she asked Joan.

Joan shook her head.

"Maybe you should go on home," my mom said, backing away from the picnic table.

"I won't let Helen hit you again. I promise," Joan said. She fingered the bottles of nail polish.

"Don't touch those," my mom snapped.

Joan's hand dropped.

My mom inched her way over to the babies' pool. She picked up the babies, and they began to cry.

"I think you girls should go home now," she said, backing away.

"You don't want to talk to me," Joan said softly.

My mom opened the screen door and took the babies inside her house.

"Go home, Joan," my mom said through the screen door. She slammed the door shut.

Joan sat at the picnic table with her head down. I put my shoes on and walked over to her. I knew she was hurt, and I wanted to punch my mom again. But I thought we ought to just leave.

"Come on, Joan, before she calls the sheriff," I whispered. Inside the house, the babies still cried.

Joan stood up. She looked at the bottles of nail polish. They glistened in the sun. Joan knocked them all down except one. She put the bright red one in her pocket.

"Come on," I said again.

Joan followed me across the yard. I flipped the babies' pool over, and the water drained out of it. I pulled it across the hot driveway.

"What are you going to do with that?" Joan asked.

"I'm going to destroy it." I wanted to hurt someone, and since my mom loved her new babies more than us, they would suffer.

Joan smiled. "No evil empress is going to stop us," Joan said in her fake French accent, and she began to sing again.

The pool made a thumping sound against the railroad tracks. We took it to the swimming hole, pushed it downstream, and ran home.

When we got home, Grandpa was mowing the yard, and my dad sat on the porch roof. He had a hammer in his hand, but he wasn't using it. He just sat there facing the sun. His eyes were closed, and his legs were crossed. I went upstairs and stood in the doorway of his room. The room was so small that it only fit a single bed and my dad's gym bag. I didn't see any spiders. I crawled onto the bed and stuck my head out the window.

Squares of roofing lay in rows around my dad. He just hadn't put any nails in them.

"Hello, Helen," my dad said.

I jumped. I didn't know that he knew I was behind him.

"Hello."

"Been to see your mom again?"

I didn't say anything.

"You went down the tracks and didn't come back wet, so I figured you went to see your mom."

I ran my finger over the dust on the windowsill.

"Come on out," he said, looking over his shoulder. He wasn't wearing a shirt, and I could see the skull on his back.

I inched my way over the windowsill. The roof was hot under my hands and knees. I sat down behind my dad. He was close to the edge, and I didn't want to go that far out. He had his eyes closed again and was facing the sun.

"So, what did she say to Joan?"

I played with the little squares of roofing.

My dad sighed, and then he got up on his knees and turned to face me. I could see the ugly red scar up close now. I wondered how he got it.

"Here." My dad handed me the hammer and a box of nails. "See those squares? Hammer them in place like this." He showed me how to hammer one then sat back down to face the sun.

The hammer felt heavy in my hand. I began to hammer the squares in. The hammer made a loud thumping sound each time I hit the wood. Some of the nails went in crooked. By the time my arm got tired, I had finished ten squares. My dad looked at the squares and smiled.

"Good job," he said. This made me feel good. He took the hammer from my hand and began pounding the rest of the squares. When he hit the nails, the bedroom window rattled. I crawled back onto the windowsill to get out of his way. His long hair was out of its ponytail and hanging in his eyes. When he was done, he faced the sun again. My dad's hair hung down his back. I could see the skull beneath it. I wondered about the skull. Where'd he get it? How long had he had it?

I crawled back out onto the roof. The new squares felt rough on my legs.

"She told Joan to go home," I whispered. "She didn't want us there."

"I know, Helen. I know." My dad reached back and patted my tennis shoe.

"I ain't never going back there." I leaned forward and put my head against my dad's back right where the tattoo was. My dad didn't move, and we sat like that until the sheriff showed up.

The sheriff's car came speeding into the yard. The siren was on, and the lights were flashing. My dad stood up, and I crawled back toward the window. The sheriff jumped out of his car followed by Joe Williams whose gun was clenched in his hands. Joe's eyes were nervously bouncing around beneath his thick eyeglasses.

"Get the hell down here!" the sheriff shouted up at my dad.

"Go inside, Helen," my dad said to me. I crawled over the windowsill and across the bed. I ran down the stairs. Joan was at the bottom of the stairs. I could tell she was scared because she looked like she was going to cry. She held my hand while we waited for my dad who walked slowly down the stairs. He had a cigarette in his clenched fist. We followed him outside where Grandpa stood on the porch steps.

"Harvey," Grandpa said to the sheriff. "What's going on here?"

"Stay out of this, George," the sheriff growled. He looked at my dad. "You son of a bitch!" The sheriff's face was red and sweating. "You keep your god-damn kids away from my wife!"

"If something has happened with the girls, it's my responsibility, not Samson's. I'm their legal guardian," Grandpa said.

Grandpa wore a black shirt with a sky-blue bird painted on the back. His pants were sky-blue. Joan had left her red shoes in the yard, and a spider was making a web inside them.

"George, shut up!" The siren of the sheriff's car screeched until Joe Williams reached into the car and turned it off. He never put down his gun or took his rapidly moving eyes off my dad and the sheriff.

My dad stepped forward into the yard, and I followed him. Joan let go of my hand and moved closer to Grandpa.

"Samson," Grandpa warned.

A Barbie doll lay naked by the sheriff's feet. The sheriff stood on one of Barbie's gowns. The purple sequins shone in the sun.

"Harvey," Grandpa said, "I got rights, and I got the right to tell you to get off my property. Unless you got some legal reason to be here, I'm telling you to leave."

"What about the fact that these two little brats stole my kids' swimming pool?" Spit flew from the sheriff's mouth. Joan and I looked at each other, and my dad looked down at me.

"Do you have any proof?" my dad asked.

"You son of a bitch!" The sheriff stepped forward and shoved my dad. It didn't seem to have much of an effect on my dad, but my dad was backing away from the sheriff.

"Fight me!" the sheriff screamed.

Things were getting crazy. The sheriff was crazy. I was scared, and I wondered what my dad would do.

"Harvey," Joe Williams said softly. "I think we should go." He slid his gun back into his holster.

The sheriff pulled the gun from his holster, pulled back the hammer, and placed it against my dad's chest right over the red scar. "I'll put a bullet in you, motherfucker." He moved the gun over my dad's heart. "This time, I'll make sure it kills you." My dad did not move.

What was he talking about? Had he shot my dad before?

"Harvey," Grandpa said frightened. "Don't do this, Harvey."

My dad rolled the cigarette that he had carried with him from upstairs between his fingers. He did not seem frightened. He seemed like he was waiting for something. "Harvey, I think you might be doing a little too much talking right now."

Grandpa was breathing with short, heavy gasps.

Joan was on the porch behind me. I couldn't see her, but I could hear her crying. My hands shook, and my legs trembled.

"Take the girls inside, Dad," my dad said to Grandpa.

"Samson," Grandpa whispered.

"Your precious girls, your precious girls," the sheriff said, "You're so protective of your poor sweet girls." The sheriff was smiling without showing his teeth.

I stood beside my dad. My glasses slid down my nose.

I heard the screen door slam, and I knew that Grandpa and Joan were inside the house.

"How noble of you, Sonny," the sheriff said.

I put my hand into one of the belt loops of my dad's jeans.

Sweat dripped from the sheriff's dark hair.

"This has nothing to do with my kids," my dad said. "This is our unfinished business."

The sheriff's car lights were still flashing. They seemed to be bouncing off of everything in the yard. The spider's web inside Joan's shoe was getting bigger and bigger.

"Wrong, Samson. This is about all of us."

The sheriff moved the gun from my dad's chest and pointed it at my forehead. I did not move. I felt my dad's weight shift toward me. The sheriff's badge glared in the sun, and I could smell his cologne. His shirt was wet with sweat, and there was a scratch on his hand.

"Harvey, this is wrong." Joe Williams muttered. "I don't want no part of this. She's just a kid. This is insane."

My dad breathed heavily. I could hear Joan crying from inside the house.

I heard the click of another gun.

Joe Williams stopped muttering, and the sheriff drew in a sharp breath.

"Now, Harvey, I really think that this has gone far enough." It was Uncle Jack.

"Jackson, this has nothing to do with you," the sheriff said; his voice was shaky. The sheriff lowered his gun. I looked up at my dad, and he was looking at Uncle Jack.

"Harrison shot you, not Samson," Uncle Jack said. "Isn't it enough that you killed Harrison?"

The sheriff laughed weakly. "It was in the line of duty. I was doing my duty."

"Get back in your car. I guarantee my nieces will stay away from your wife."

"You said that before," the sheriff said.

"I'll make absolutely certain this time," Uncle Jack said. There was a warning in Uncle Jack's voice that I wasn't going to ignore this time.

The sheriff put his gun back into its holster and walked to his car. He stumbled over Barbie's van. "You can't put a gun to a police officer's head and get away with it," he muttered.

"What gun? Harvey, I have no idea what you are talking about. Do you?" Uncle Jack asked Joe Williams. Uncle Jack still pointed the gun at the sheriff. It was a hunting rifle. I had never seen it before. Uncle Jack's glasses slid down his nose. He wore a black suit with a yellow tie.

"No sir, I do not," Joe Williams said. He climbed into the driver's side of the sheriff's car making the sheriff sit on the passenger side. He turned off the lights then backed the car out of the yard. The sheriff glared at us.

Uncle Jack put the gun into my dad's hand.
"It's not loaded," he said, his hands shaking.
My dad laughed loudly and reached out to hug Uncle Jack.

CHAPTER 8

GRANDMA'S GOLD CHAIR HAD DISAPPEARED FROM THE FRONT YARD, SO I FIGURED someone had thrown it away until I saw it sitting in the living room of her and Billy Jacobs' trailer. I didn't know how she got it. But there it was in the living room of her small, ugly, olive-green trailer. I didn't know what happened to the rug with the red stain.

The trailer had a tin roof, and when no one was home, I threw rocks and rotten apples against it. It made a nice clanging sound like two pots banging together.

I liked to watch Grandma's house. It made me feel like a spy. I knew what days she did her laundry because I could see it hanging from her clothesline. I knew that she drove a little blue car that rattled when she pulled into the driveway.

I suppose I wanted to catch her at something, but she never did anything except argue with Billy. I could hear her voice from inside the trailer. It was a loud screeching sound. She screamed at Billy a lot, but Billy never said anything back, at least, anything I could hear.

I just couldn't figure it out. If you couldn't take a piss in this town without everyone knowing it, how come I didn't know about my grandma and Billy? How had they kept it from me? You'd think those blabbermouths the Maxwell's would have told it. I sighed. Obviously, if you're a kid, you didn't always know who was pissing in this town.

I wanted to walk right up to my grandma's door and tell her what I really thought of her taking off and of her showing up again and being mean to Joan and, well, everyone else. But I guess I figured there was no point. She would probably just react like my mom had, and I'd have to punch her, too, and punching my mom had only gotten me in trouble, and I promised Uncle Jack I'd stay out of trouble. I didn't tell Uncle Jack this, but even before the gun incident, I had decided that I wasn't going anywhere near my mom again. Not because I was worried about being in trouble but because I was worried that Joan's feelings would be hurt again. I could take the fact that she didn't want me; after all, I was like my dad, but Joan couldn't understand her being so mean.

I suppose I should have been scared about the sheriff putting his gun to my head. I was, when it happened, but now it seemed like my Uncle Jack had it under control, and it seemed like Joe had taken away some of the sheriff's power. It didn't matter anyway because I wasn't going back to their house again. I didn't need anything there anymore.

I sat in the apple tree by my grandma's house thinking about this when Billy Jacobs caught me.

"You shouldn't be spying on people," he said, looking up at me.

"I wasn't spying," I lied. "I was just lookin'."

"What are you looking for?"

"I'm not lookin' for anything. I'm just lookin'."

"Well, I think you better get out of that tree and go on home before your grandma gets back."

I slid down a few branches to get a better look at him. He wore a pair of jeans and a faded flannel shirt. There were holes at the elbows of the shirt. From up in the tree, he looked small.

"What's she going to do to me?" I demanded.

"Well, you stay up there awhile, and you'll find out."

"You scared of her?" I asked. I slid down another branch. Apples fell from the tree, and Billy stepped back to avoid them.

"You should be scared of her. She likes to get her own way."

"Why do you stay with her if she's mean to you?"

Billy shrugged and climbed up the tree to meet me. I retreated until two branches separated us.

"So, what do you do up here?" he asked.

I shrugged.

He took a rotting apple and tossed it against the tin roof.

"You know, rotten eggs make a great sound against a tin roof, plus the stink is so bad that the people in the house have to climb up on their roof and spray the eggs off of it."

Why would he tell me that? He knew I'd try it the first chance I got. He was definitely setting me up.

"You going to rat on me?" I asked.

"Nah," Billy said, tossing another apple. It splattered against the roof.

"Why not?" I tossed an apple, too. It bounced off the roof and landed in the yard by their front door.

"Your grandma will step on that for sure," he said with a grin. "I'm serious about you heading home. Ain't nothing here for you except more of her mean shit. She won't tell you nothing anyway."

"What makes you think I want to know something?"

"Come on, you've been sitting in this tree every day for two weeks, watching and waiting for something."

Billy hung upside down. His shirt flew up, showing his belly. When he sat up, his face was red. "I'm telling you. You won't find answers here."

"Well, if I can't find out here, I can't find out anywhere."

"Maybe it's better not to know."

"Sometimes you have to know."

Billy tossed another apple. "How old are you?" he asked.

"12," I said.

He nodded. "I figured. When I was 12, my old man disappeared. I didn't know why. One person told me one story. Another person, another story. So, when you ain't got a sure thing to blame it on, you blame it on yourself. Then, I grew up and realized some people are just selfish. When they want to move on, they move on, and there ain't a damn thing a kid can do about it."

He climbed down from the tree because Grandma's car was coming down the road.

"Go on home now. Don't come back. But, if you have to come back, bring some rotten eggs," he said grinning. "I'll have to clean them off the roof eventually, but it will drive her crazy until I do."

I climbed down from the tree and headed home.

When I got home, my dad was sitting on the front porch swing with Joan.

Joan had a book in her hand and was explaining the story to our dad. "The ducks aren't really ducks. They are princesses who were turned into ducks by the evil witch."

My dad smiled and nodded as he listened to Joan, and I sat on the porch steps and listened, too. I knew the story. It was a book for babies, but Joan liked the story, so we played magic ducks a lot.

"The witch wanted the princesses' gold and jewelry, but they wouldn't give it to her. So she turned them into ducks and the only way they can be princesses again is if a handsome prince kisses them."

"Do princes usually kiss ducks?" my dad asked.

"No, these are magic ducks. They can talk and tell the prince what's wrong, and he can help them."

"What if he doesn't want to help?"

Joan looked frustrated. "A prince always helps." She stood up from the swing and put her hands on her hips. "You should read more books." She went inside, slamming the screen door behind her.

My dad laughed.

"So, Helen, do you believe the prince always helps?" he asked me.

"Nope."

"Me neither," he said. He began to rock the swing.

"So, where you been keeping yourself lately?" he asked.

"I've been around," I said, hoping I sounded as cool as he did.

We sat there in silence. The wind blew. Joan's red shoes weren't in the yard anymore.

"How did Grandma get her gold chair back?" I asked.

The swing stopped, and my dad chuckled. "You don't miss a thing, do you? You've been spying on your grandma?"

I said nothing.

"Your grandpa gave it to her."

"Why?"

"Sometimes, the prince still loves the wicked witch," my dad said, patting my head as he stood up from the swing and walked into the house.

CHAPTER 9

Uncle Jack gave my dad a job with his landscaping business. Sometimes, Joan and I got to work with them. Uncle Jack had two other employees, Eddie Clayton and his uncle, Fizzy. Eddie was six-foot-five and nineteen years old. He had a mass of long, dark, curly hair and a scar on his dark face that ran from the corner of his eye to the corner of his mouth. Eddie had a white mom and a black dad that nobody had ever seen.

Fizzy was a fifty-year-old white guy who looked like he was seventy. His hands shook because he drank too much. Eddie had an older brother named Vince who was always in and out of jail. When he was out, Uncle Jack gave him a job. I learned all this by listening to Uncle Jack and my dad talk as we drove from one job site to another.

Today, Joan and I rode in the back of Uncle Jack's landscaping truck. We were pressed into a corner behind the mowers and the bags of fertilizer. Joan rested her head on my knee. Eddie sat near the tailgate with his back to us. Uncle Jack, my dad, and Fizzy sat up front in the cab. Joan hummed.

Today, we were going to the clothing factory in Meyersdale. We had been there several times before. The women who worked there ate lunch outside and watched my dad and Uncle Jack. Sometimes, they would offer Joan and me candy to tell them things about my dad and Uncle Jack. We weren't sure if we were allowed to take the candy.

When we got to the factory, we climbed out of the truck over the mowers, fertilizer, and trees. Eddie always opened the tailgate for us and helped us down from the truck, but he never said anything to us.

Joan and I waited in the grass with Fizzy while Eddie, Uncle Jack, and my dad unloaded the truck. Fizzy always messed up our names, so he called us buttercup or sweetheart or angel pie or any other silly name that came to mind.

"Well, Dumplings," he said, putting a shaking hand on Joan's head. "Time to get to work."

He went to help Eddie with a bag of fertilizer.

Joan stood next to me. Her fingernails were painted bright red. She had used the nail polish she stole from our mom.

The women from the factory walked out the door for lunch. A roar of talk and giggles began as soon as they spotted my dad and Uncle Jack, who had already begun mowing. Eddie used the weed eater around the side of the building. Fizzy and I pulled weeds from a row of flowerbeds next to the factory sign. Joan stood staring at the women, and I pulled her arm and made her kneel down beside me. "They don't need to know anything about Uncle Jack and Sonny," I whispered.

"Right you are, Sugar Melon," Fizzy said smiling. "Unless they offer you something good." Fizzy was missing his two front teeth. "Watch this," he said, standing up. He put his butt in the air and wiggled it. This brought a roar of laughter and a few disgusted groans from the women. My dad pushed a mower past us and shook his finger at Fizzy.

"I'm hungry. Go on over there," Fizzy said, "and get us some of them snack cakes. Tell 'em all about me."

I looked at him, trying to decide if he was serious. "Go on," he said.

I nodded and walked over to the picnic tables where the women ate and smoked cigarettes. They were quiet as I approached.

"Hello," one of them said. By now, I knew their game. They would smile and coo and ask if I wanted anything to eat. I decided to avoid this.

"I've got information that I'll trade for snack cakes," I declared.

Immediately, snack cakes came flying down the picnic table. "What do you want to know?" I asked.

"The big one with the long hair. What's his name?" one of them asked. The women started to giggle again.

"That's my dad," I said. "His name is Samson."

They laughed and made comments about Delilah. I knew who Delilah was. Every Wednesday night, we went to church. Uncle Jack still preached on Wednesday nights. He wanted to quit, but there wasn't anyone else to take his place. Besides, folks in the church liked Uncle Jack. They hugged him and made him pies and cakes.

Last week in the bathroom of the church, I heard Mrs. White tell Mrs. Gardner, "I don't care if he's queer or not. He stayed up with me all night when Fred had a stroke. And that was more than that skirt-chasing Reverend Paine has ever done."

"Where's your mom?" One of the factory women asked.

I scooped up the cakes in my arms. "She married someone else after my dad went to prison."

I walked away. I knew the prison story would keep them interested for a while. They began to talk even louder.

"Is that Samson Cooper?"

"You remember his brother, Harrison, got killed."

"Well, prison has been good to him."

I handed Fizzy the snack cakes. He grinned.

"What did you tell them?" Joan asked.

"Just some stuff." It was stuff I was sure they already knew anyway. We ate the cakes, saving some of them for Uncle Jack, my dad, and Eddie.

"Hey, little girl," one of the women called to me. She waved a soda can.

I looked at Fizzy.

"Got to have something to drink," he shrugged.

I stood up and walked over to the table. Several soda cans slid down the table toward me.

"What do you want to know?" I asked, picking up the cans of soda.

"That one." They pointed at Uncle Jack.

"That's Uncle Jack," I said. "He's a preacher. He wouldn't be interested in any of you."

I didn't say it was because he didn't like women, so they got mad at me.

"Leave Helen alone, you bunch of harlots," a hunchbacked old woman growled. She sat against the wall of the factory, smoking a cigarette. The sun shone on her. Her face was wrinkled, and there were places on her head where her pink scalp showed beneath her hair. I looked at her as the other women went back to whispering about my dad.

"Come here and sit down, Helen," she said. She patted the grass next to her, and I went and sat down beside her. There was a big black purse on the ground between us.

"How do you know my name?"

"I know lots of things."

I thought maybe she was a witch or crazy, or maybe you couldn't take a secret piss in Meyersdale either.

I looked into the purse. It had two bags from the drug store, several different colored cigarette lighters, balls of Kleenex, a blue wallet stuffed with receipts, and envelopes wrapped with rubber bands.

"Well, you certainly look like your daddy. Not a trace of your mother in you," she said, eyeing me up and down.

"You know my dad?" I asked.

"Yes, and I knew your mom, too." She reached into her purse and pulled out a pack of cigarettes and a black lighter with a silver eagle on it. She seemed to forget about the cigarette that hung from her lips. I wondered if she was going to smoke two cigarettes at once. I wondered what was in the envelopes.

"Louise was such a beauty," the hunchback woman muttered.

The hunchbacked woman reached inside one of her drug store bags and pulled out a large green pill. She popped the pill into her mouth. I watched her swallow the pill without water.

"Who's Louise?" I wondered if she took those pills because she was crazy.

"My daughter. She got killed on the railroad tracks by our house."

"Mr. Coolie said his daughter got killed on the railroad tracks, too."

I could hear Fizzy laughing and the sound of the weed eater.

"I went a little crazy after Louise's death. I was in no condition to raise a baby."

I knew I was right about her being crazy, but now I wondered how crazy.

"What baby?" I asked.

The hunchbacked lady patted me on the head. "Not a trace of your mother in you."

I sat very still next to her as she stared at me. She wasn't making sense, and the soda cans felt cold against my arm.

"What baby?" I asked again.

She didn't answer me. She had crushed the first cigarette in the grass and was smoking a new one. She didn't smoke like my dad. She took long puffs and held the cigarette tight between her lips. I figured she was really crazy.

Uncle Jack called my name. Most of the factory women had gone back inside.

"Well, I got to go," I said standing up. "Maybe I can hear about the baby some other time."

Uncle Jack came striding toward me.

"What was the baby's name?" I asked. I watched Fizzy and Eddie lifting the mowers onto the truck.

"Helen," she said as she struggled up from the ground. Uncle Jack smiled as he walked toward me. When he saw the old woman, he stopped smiling. He was shocked.

"Hello, Jackson."

"Hello, Helen," he said to her.

Uncle Jack didn't look at me as he took some of the soda cans from my hands. We walked toward the truck, and the old lady walked into the factory. I turned to look at her.

Uncle Jack led me to the truck and lifted me into the bed of the truck. Joan and Eddie ate snack cakes and hummed. They seemed to be humming the same song. I leaned my head against the side of the truck. I just couldn't understand what the old woman was talking about, and why was Uncle Jack so upset? And why did the old woman have the same name as me? Uncle Jack's eyes shone from the rearview mirror as he watched me.

When we got home, Uncle Jack helped me down from the truck. "I think you and I should take a walk."

I nodded. My dad looked confused.

We walked down the railroad tracks. Mr. Coolie's cat followed us until something in the weeds caught his attention. At the swimming hole, Uncle Jack took off his boots and waded at the edge of the water. We both tossed rocks into the water.

"I guess you have a lot of questions," he said.

"Who is she?" I watched the rocks bounce across the water and fall out of sight.

"Helen Coolie. She was married to Mr. Coolie." His voice cracked. "Everyone was a mess, especially your dad," he paused. "Then he married Amy, and everyone thought it would be easier to just not tell you."

Uncle Jack's voice broke off. His toes moved softly and quietly through the water.

I was pissed. "Tell me what?"

Uncle Jack sighed. "The Coolie's are your grandparents. Their daughter's name was Louise. We called her Lou. She was your mother."

"Amy is my mom," I said.

"No," Uncle Jack shook his head. "Amy is Joan's mom. Lou was your mother." He bent down to pick up his boots.

I was pissed. Why hadn't they told me about her? Was she crazy like her mom, that Helen lady? Maybe that's why they decided not to tell me about her.

I heard a train whistle, and I remembered Mr. Coolie saying that his daughter had been killed on the railroad tracks, and I knew why they hadn't told me.

"She died on the railroad tracks," I said. I let the rocks I was holding drop into the water.

"Yes," Uncle Jack said. "It was an accident. We were drinking, and she insisted on walking home by herself."

"She got hit by a train?" I asked.

"We don't know. The coroner said it was possible that she fell and hit her head and never felt the train."

I looked at Uncle Jack, and he looked at me. Neither of us believed that story.

The train whistle blew again, closer this time, and I wondered what it felt like to get hit by a train. I wondered what it felt like to die.

The hot wind from the train blew against our faces and arms as it passed by us.

I'd never thought Uncle Jack liked me, but he reached out and took my hand. I held onto his hand.

CHAPTER 10

That night, when everyone was in bed, I heard my dad walk into Grandpa's room. I was lying beside Joan who was hugging her one-eyed monkey. We had never found the missing eye, and the monkey's tail kept falling off, but Grandpa kept sewing it back on. Joan never played with it, but she couldn't sleep without it. My dad said good night to Grandpa and walked down the hall to his room.

I waited until Grandpa's breathing was replaced by his wheezing snore then climbed out of bed. Joan moved slightly but did not wake up. The monkey fell on the floor.

I walked down the hall. A train whistle blew. I stood still, waiting to feel the vibrations under my feet. I wore a white nightgown, and sweat dripped down my back. I pushed open the door to my dad's room. It was dark, but I could see the glow of his cigarette. He was outside on the roof. The train passed, and everything was silent again. I stood in the doorway and watched the glow of my dad's cigarette. When he crushed it out, everything was dark again.

"Come out here, Helen," my dad whispered.

I was startled. I felt my way in the dark room over the bed and onto the windowsill. My dad pulled me out onto a blanket that he was sitting on.

"How did you know I was standing there?"

He shrugged. I saw his large shoulders move in the dark.

"Why are you out here?"

"I was thinking."

"About what?"

A warm breeze blew across the porch roof. I wished for the train because it was too quiet. Fireflies flew around the roof. I could make out their tiny glow in the dark.

My dad sighed. "Lies."

He said it so soft that I wasn't sure if I heard it, and if I heard it, I wasn't so sure I wanted to hear it. I sat behind my dad. I knew the skull was on his back, but I couldn't see it in the dark.

"We shouldn't have lied to you," my dad said.

I agreed. I wanted to ask a million questions about my mom. Who was she? What did she look like? But 'why did you lie" was the only question that came out of my mouth.

"It was easier. I guess. Losing Lou was," his voice cracked like he was going to cry, and he paused. "It was hard. It was the moment that broke everything apart. Nothing was the same after that. I was angry at myself, at her, at the world."

There were several bats circling the house now, and they scared me. The sky was black. Mr. Coolie's cat ran through the yard, his eyes shining in the darkness. I rested my head against my dad's back, and his hair felt soft against my cheek.

My dad watched the bats. "We were out of control. Old Man Coolie had a fishing cabin on Savage Mountain. It started out with just rebuilding cars. You know, something to do, and then Lou died, and things got out of control."

My dad stopped talking and took a deep breath. I didn't know if he'd keep talking or if I even wanted him to. I wondered about my mother, this Lou who had left everyone so broken.

"Everyone just thought it was easier. We just stopped talking about Lou. I guess we figured a scar don't hurt as much as an open wound, or so we thought. I knew coming back here would be a reckoning. All my actions good and bad would be judged, and I would be punished accordingly."

"You sound like Grandma," I said.

He chuckled. "I guess something from all of those church meetings sank in. And Lord knows that woman is part of my reckoning. She's already been judge and jury. Now, she wants to be my executioner."

He lit a cigarette. A train whistle blew, and the house shook. I leaned my face against the skull tattoo and put my arms around my dad. The scar felt rough under my fingers as I hugged him. I waited for the rest of the story, but after the train had gone, my dad's mood had changed.

"It's late, Helen," he said. "Go on to bed."

I wanted to argue, to demand the rest of the story, but my dad had gone as silent as stone keeping himself to himself, and I crawled back through the bedroom window.

CHAPTER 11

When my dad got his paycheck, he took us to Somerset to eat at the diner. We ate cheeseburgers. It was hot outside, and a fan spun around over our heads. Our legs stuck to the bright red booths. Grandpa was eating a BBQ ham sandwich. The ham kept sliding out of the bun and onto Grandpa's plate. Grandpa shoved the ham back into his sandwich, and a stack of napkins began to pile up at his elbow.

The waitress kept coming over to smile at my dad. Her nametag said 'Missy'. Joan wore a green dress with a frog on the front of it. The frog's eyes moved every time she giggled.

When the door of the diner opened, a little silver bell chimed. Uncle Jack walked into the diner. He wore a black baseball cap, t-shirt, and jeans. Behind Uncle Jack was a short, bearded man dressed in jeans and a t-shirt. I knew from the pictures that he was Alex Coolie. I also knew he was my uncle. I looked at his face, trying to see if we looked alike. We didn't. I still hadn't seen a picture of my mom, so I wasn't sure if I looked like her, but I was sure I looked like my dad and not Alex Coolie.

Alex walked by dad and patted his shoulder. "Good to see you, Samson."

My dad grinned. "You too, Alex. You, too."

The little silver bell chimed again, and Mr. Coolie walked in. He wore a pair of bib overalls and no shirt.

"Now, Paul," one of the waitresses shouted at Mr. Coolie. "You know you can't come in here without a shirt."

"Hey," Mr. Coolie said to me, ignoring the waitress.

"Hey," I said.

I looked at Mr. Coolie. I tried to see myself in him. But I couldn't. I looked at Joan, and she looked at me. Her elbows rested on the table, and her chin rested on her fists.

I looked around the room. I now had another grandfather, another uncle, and somewhere there was another grandma, taking her pills. I half expected her to appear in the diner, too. Everything in my world had changed like someone had thrown the pieces of a puzzle on the table, and I was expected to put them together, only I couldn't see the picture on the front of the box to find out exactly where I fit. A drop of sweat slid down my back.

The waitress reported Mr. Coolie to the manager, and the manager started to walk toward us. He saw my dad, stopped, turned around, and told the waitress to let it go.

Fizzy and Eddie walked into the diner. Mr. Coolie put his arm around Alex and made a silly face at him. The waitress moved tables, so we could all sit together. Eddie helped her, and Uncle Jack laughed at something Fizzy said.

When the silver bell rang again, my old grandma walked in wearing a purple tube top and a purple mini-skirt. Her lipstick was bright purple. She looked like she smelled something rotten and didn't like it. I thought about Billy and the eggs on the roof. I hadn't done it yet, but someday, I would.

Everyone was quiet. Grandpa's back stiffened, and he slid his plate away from him. My grandma narrowed her eyes when she looked at my dad. My dad shifted in the booth, and I looked out the window. Billy Jacobs waited in his Jeep.

"What do you want?" my dad asked.

"I was driving by, and I saw you were all in here having a family reunion." She looked at Alex Coolie with disgust and made a grunting sound in her throat. Then she looked at me. "Guess the cat's out of the bag, Helen. Look at you with your other family."

I hadn't told Joan about my mom yet. She looked confused. I was mad at my grandma for saying anything about it.

I said nothing, and my grandma's eyes narrowed at me the same way they narrowed at my dad. "It's not polite to ignore an adult when they're talking to you."

Grandma carried a large purple purse, and she tapped Grandpa in the arm with it. "Ain't that right, George?"

Grandpa nodded.

My dad watched the purple purse as Grandma twisted the handle in her hands.

Grandpa did not look at Grandma but stared at the table.

"What do you want?" my dad asked again.

"I thought I'd come in here and say hi to the girls," she said.

It was a lie, and everyone knew it.

"That all right with you, George, if I say hi to the girls."

Grandpa said nothing.

"I said is that all right," Grandma said. She went to hit Grandpa with the purse again, but my dad reached out and stopped the purse.

Grandma looked at my dad. "So, that's how it is." She looked at Grandpa. "You never gave a damn about Harrison, and now you're sitting across from the thief that killed him."

"Sonny didn't kill Harrison," Grandpa said.

"He got Harrison involved in all that mess."

I felt my dad shift in the booth again.

"It was always this way," Grandma hissed at Grandpa. "You always favorited these two over my Harrison."

Grandpa shook his head. Grandma's hand came down hard against Grandpa's arm. The smacking sound echoed through the diner. Grandpa didn't move, but my dad stood up.

"Sit down, Samson," Grandpa said. He looked at Grandma for the first time since she had come into the diner. "I loved Harrison," Grandpa said. "I love all my sons."

"Love. What do you know about love, you old fool? Blind in love with me for years and every one of those years, I ran around on you." Grandma hissed the words at Grandpa. Her hand went up to strike Grandpa again. I jumped up and stood between Grandma's hand and Grandpa. Her hand came down hard across the side of my head. It hurt, but I didn't move or say anything. The thud echoed through the diner, and Grandma looked at my dad.

"This is your fault," she said to my dad. She slung the purse over her shoulder and walked away. The little silver bell rang as she walked out of the diner. I followed her out onto the sidewalk. Heat waves rose up from it.

She opened the door of Billy's Jeep, looked back, and saw me. Her face was twisted with anger.

"Why did you come here?" I asked her.

She climbed into the jeep and slammed the door. "It's none of your god-damn business," she said. I saw her look through the window into the diner at my dad.

"I'm going to get that son of a bitch," she hissed to Billy, and I remembered what my dad said about her being his executioner.

Billy Jacobs pulled the Jeep away from the curb.

I went back inside. Everyone was sitting at the big table now. Alex Coolie touched my hand as I walked past him.

CHAPTER 12

"Keep your voice down, Samson."

Grandpa's voice woke me.

"All I'm saying is they need to respect other people's privacy." My dad's voice was deep and angry.

"They're curious about you."

I smelled coffee and heard Grandpa pouring it into his cup. Grandpa's favorite cup was shaped like a cowboy boot.

"Well, I don't want them going through my things." My dad's voice was scratchy and mean.

"I'll talk to them, but it's just some letters and photos."

"It's more than that."

"What do you mean more than that?" Grandpa's voice was loud and angry. "What is it, Samson? What do you have up there that is such a secret? Because if it's drugs, you can get the hell out now." I had heard Grandpa mad before, but he never sounded like this. It made me nervous. I heard a chair squeak across the floor.

"It's not drugs."

"It better not be. I've had enough of that shit. I may not have raised you boys the best, but them girls upstairs are good girls, and I want them to stay that way. I made a promise after your mother left that I wasn't going to let them down."

"You mean like I did. Don't you?"

"I ain't said that."

"You didn't have to, Dad. I get the point."

"You better choose your battles, Samson. Them girls are getting attached to you, but it's a thin string that can break easily."

My dad grunted, and I heard the click of his lighter.

Grandpa banged dishes around in the cupboard, and I heard spoons drop onto the table. "And take that goddamn cigarette outside!"

The chair squeaked, and my dad slammed the front door. Grandpa breathed heavily. I climbed out of bed. I was glad that Joan wasn't awake.

Later, my dad drove us to school. Grandpa never took us to school. We always rode the bus. The sky was filled with clouds making everything dark. I sat in the back seat, and Joan was in the front seat, talking fast. My dad wore a baseball hat and looked grumpy. He drank coffee from a dirty plastic red mug. "Quikfill" was written on the mug in fading white letters. We crossed the railroad tracks, and the bottom of the car scraped against them.

"It does that all the time. Grandpa says it's the muffler," Joan said.

We pulled up in front of the school. Joan hugged and kissed my dad. She called him daddy then got out of the car and ran into the building. I sat there staring at the back of my dad's head.

"What are you waiting for, Helen? Go on." His voice was still scratchy. He looked at me through the rearview mirror, and I glared at him. "What's your problem?" he asked.

"I was in your stuff, not Joan. If you're going to be mean to anyone, be mean to me."

My dad sounded annoyed. "I'm not going to be mean to anyone."

"You were already mean to Grandpa." I got out of the car and slammed the door.

Most of the day, I was mad. I ate lunch, but I didn't feel like it. My bad stomachache had come back, and I didn't like this new side of my dad. He had said he was mad at the world after my mom died. Was he still mad? If he was angry with my mom, was he angry with me, too?

What did he have in the bag? I don't think Joan ever got to look at everything. Or was there something new? What was he hiding?

Outside on the playground, the sky was still gray and black, but it hadn't rained yet. Usually, I played on the swings, but today, I just leaned against the building.

I was mad at myself for acting like Joan, thinking he was really going to be my dad. I was mad at myself for thinking I could trust him. I was mad because I had written to him in the first place. If I hadn't written to him, maybe he wouldn't have come back, and there would be no trouble with my grandmother or the sheriff. I was mad at him and all the other lying adults.

Mark and Mitch Maxwell walked toward me with Timmy Gilbert, who was nervous. Timmy was always nervous and afraid of everything. In first grade, he peed his pants when the firemen came to visit, and they blew the fire whistle. Once when a bee came into the classroom, he cried so hard he had to go home.

"Hey," Mitch Maxwell said.

"Hey, Helen," Mark said. "Tell Timmy that your dad's out of prison. He doesn't believe us."

I knew they were being mean to Timmy because he always thought there was someone waiting to get him.

"Yeah," I said.

Timmy began to fidget. "They let him out?"

"Sure," I said. "They let him out. He did his time." I was trying to sound like one of the cops on TV.

"Tell Timmy what your dad did to go to prison," Mitch said. Suddenly, it was hard to tell them apart because they were both mean and ugly.

I wanted to be mean, too. I wanted to say horrible things. I wanted to make Timmy cry or pee his pants or something.

Thunder banged, and Timmy jumped.

"My dad went to prison because he shoplifted."

The clouds rumbled. Mitch Maxwell swallowed hard. The Maxwell's were always shoplifting at the drug store, and they didn't know I knew until now.

"I don't shoplift," Timmy said. He ran toward Miss Mason.

"That's not what he went to prison for," Mitch said.

"And you better not say nothin' to nobody," Mark warned me.

Suddenly, I was so mad that I saw red. The sky was red. The playground was red, and so was Mark's ugly face. I reached out and grabbed Mark by the front of his shirt and slammed him against the wall. "Don't threaten me."

We heard Miss Mason call us inside because recess was over. The Maxwell's ran for the door, and I smiled.

CHAPTER 13

Our bedroom was dark. Joan and the purple monkey lay next to me. Joan talked in her sleep, but she muttered, and it never made any sense. The rain was hitting the roof loudly, and the wind rattled the windows. My dad wasn't home. I didn't know where he was, but I didn't care because I was still mad at him and so was Grandpa. Grandpa hadn't said that, but I knew he was. I hoped my dad had gone away for good.

I heard a knocking sound. I thought it was a tree branch hitting the window, so I rolled over and tried to ignore it. It got louder. I listened carefully, but all I heard was rain. I unwrapped one of the blankets from Joan's feet and covered my head with it. The knocking sound got louder. I wondered why Grandpa wasn't awake. I gave Joan back the blanket, got out of bed, and went out into the hallway. The knocking sound was coming from the front porch.

My dad was probably locked out. I was glad, but I knew that Grandpa would be mad if I didn't let him into the house. The light in the hallway was out, and it was hard to see anything, so I had to be careful as I walked down the stairs. I thought I heard a baby crying. I pulled back the curtain that hung over the front door and looked outside, but I couldn't see anything clearly. I turned on the porch light.

Joan's mom, Amy, stood in the doorway with her two babies. Her nose was bleeding, and there were bruises on her face. One of the babies was crying, and the other was looking around.

I don't know why, but I let them come into the house. I suppose it was because I knew Grandpa would be mad if I didn't.

"I didn't have anywhere else to go, Helen," she said. "I know I wasn't very nice to you or Joan, but I was scared. He can be so mean and …"

"You were mean to Joan and me," I said.

She started to cry. Me and the quiet baby watched her. I wasn't sure, but I thought they were real tears this time, and her face did look awful. I took the quiet baby from her arms. It looked at me as I took its wet jacket off. I went into the kitchen and turned on the light. Amy followed me.

"You walk here?" I asked her. I sat the quiet baby on the floor and gave it a Barbie doll to hold.

Amy took off the crying baby's jacket. "Yes, I couldn't get the car keys from him. He locked us in the bedroom, so I climbed out the window and came here." She talked very fast, and her hands shook. The crying baby had stopped crying and had started to suck its thumb.

"Take off your coat. I'll get Grandpa. He'll know what to do."

"No, Helen. I just need a few minutes then I'll go on home." She wiped her nose with her hand. I went over to the cupboard and got her a towel. She held it up to her bleeding nose. The baby on the floor was sucking on Barbie's hair.

"You can't go back to him. He'll hurt you more. I'll get Grandpa."

Someone was coming down the stairs. I hoped it was Grandpa and not Joan. My dad walked into the kitchen. There was silence in the kitchen as we stared at each other. I had no idea he had come home, and now, he stood in the kitchen, looking angry, and I was glad that I let Amy into the house because it made him mad.

"What the hell are you doing here?" he said to Amy.

The wind blew harder, and the rain slapped against the kitchen window. The witch was back in the clock, but she leaned to one side.

Amy looked at my dad and cried harder. They were definitely real tears this time.

"I just need a few minutes then I'll go home," Amy said softly.

My dad walked to the front door and looked outside. "He follow you?" There was a clicking sound as my dad locked the front door.

"I don't think so." Her nose was still bleeding, and I gave her an ice cube to put inside the towel. Amy was surprised. "How did you know to do that?"

"Grandpa always does it."

She smiled at me.

Grandpa came downstairs. "Good God, would you look at your face! Give me that baby, and you hold your head back to stop that bleeding." Grandpa took the baby from her arms. It didn't cry. "Helen, you get some ice and hold it on her eye. We don't want that to swell up anymore." I did what Grandpa said.

My dad was still staring out the window.

"Samson, you go upstairs and get some dry t-shirts from the girls' room. They'll be too big for the babies, but they'll be dry."

"You can't be serious. Do you know what kind of trouble this will cause?" my dad said to him.

"You sound like Uncle Jack," I said.

"Well, maybe Jack is pretty smart sometimes, and when did you get to be such a fan of hers anyway?" he said to me.

"I didn't say I liked her." The ice was melting and dripping down her face.

"Will you two stop it? She's sitting right in front of you. Stop talking like she ain't here," Grandpa said.

"Well, there'll be trouble," my dad muttered as he walked upstairs.

"He's right," Amy said. "He'll be so angry if he finds out I came here." Her nose had stopped bleeding, and she was looking at Grandpa.

"We'll handle it," Grandpa said, "Now, first thing we got to do is find a phone, call the State Police and have them file a report."

"Oh, no," Amy interrupted. "He'd kill me."

Both babies were asleep, one on the floor and one in Grandpa's arms.

"Amy, if you don't and you go back, he'll kill you for sure. Remember what you said to me about Joan."

Amy nodded. I wondered what she'd told Grandpa about Joan.

"Well, the same thing goes for these babies."

"What did you say about Joan?" I asked.

"Never you mind. You go on upstairs and bring down some towels," Grandpa said.

When I came back downstairs, my dad was standing by the door again. The babies were dressed in Joan's t-shirts. They lay together on a blanket on the living room floor. I handed some towels to Amy, and she thanked me. While I was upstairs, it was decided that my dad and I would take Amy to the hospital because the police would file a report.

Grandpa told me to go and get dressed. I did what he said. I thought my dad would argue, but he said nothing. I worried about the sheriff coming around looking for Amy. I thought he'd hurt the babies or Grandpa. What if he hurt Joan? Joan sat at the top of the stairs, hugging her legs. Her eyes were wide and bright in the darkness. I sat next to her putting on my tennis shoes.

"It will be all right," I told her.

"No, it won't. It won't ever be all right again." She started crying.

I hugged her. "Sure, it will, Joan."

"No, it won't. The sheriff won't ever leave us alone now."

I felt very scared because she was right. Everything seemed quiet now. The rain had slowed down, and I hadn't heard a train pass by since Amy had knocked on the door.

Grandpa called to me from the bottom of the stairs.

In the car, Amy sat in the backseat, shivering. I sat in the front seat next to my dad. He didn't say anything, but every once in a while, he looked in the rearview mirror.

At the hospital, my dad went outside to smoke. I sat with Amy in the examination room. The room was pale yellow, and the paint was peeling in the corner by the sink. The lights were too bright, and people talked too loud, and it smelled like bleach. Someone cried, and I wanted to go home. The nurse gave Amy a gown to wear. The nurse wore too much perfume, and her dress was too tight.

"The doctor will be here in a few minutes. We had a bad accident on the turnpike. We're kind of busy right now. I'm sure you know we called the police."

Amy nodded. She seemed small like she would disappear into the white hospital bed. The nurse walked away.

Amy took off her wet jacket and unbuttoned her blouse. Her hands shook.

"I hate hospitals," she said. "Put my coat and shirt over there, please, Helen."

I took the clothes from her. When I turned around, she had the gown on.

After a long time, a doctor appeared. He was tall and thin with glasses. He didn't look Amy in the eye.

"So, your husband hit you. Take off your gown."

Amy did what he said, but she looked like she was going to cry.

I watched. Amy was completely covered with bruises. A large black one covered her side. There were finger marks around her arm and neck.

"He choke you?" The doctor said, running his fingers over the marks.

Amy started to cry, and my dad pulled back the curtain and walked in.

The doctor looked up over the top of his glasses. "You her husband?" he asked my dad.

"No, sir. Not anymore."

The doctor's hands dropped away from Amy. He turned to look at my dad, pushing up his glasses. "I was asking if you were responsible for this."

"No, I'm not. Did she tell you I was?" My dad glared at Amy.

"She told my nurse it was her husband. I'm trying to figure out if you're that husband."

"No, sir. I'm not. And I don't think it's any of your business. I think that's for the police to decide."

The curtain pulled back, and the nurse brought in two policemen. One of them looked at my dad. "I think you need to wait outside."

My dad walked away.

"Little girl, I think you should go on outside, too," the policeman said.

"I want to stay with Amy."

"Go on now," the nurse said, touching my shoulder.

I jerked away and looked at Amy. "Are you going to be all right?"

Amy nodded.

I walked out. I followed the exit signs to the lobby. In the lobby, an old man was crying for his mother, and a little boy held his bleeding arm. Uncle Jack stood next to the soda machine, and I ran and hugged him.

CHAPTER 14

In the morning, I awoke to find the babies on the living room floor watching "Sesame Street". I had slept on the couch, and Uncle Jack was still asleep on the floor. He was curled into a ball with an afghan over him. His socks stuck out from the bottom of the afghan. He wasn't wearing his favorite baseball hat, the one with a bird on it, and the sunlight shone on his balding head.

I heard someone pouring cereal into a bowl and the sound of a train whistle. A train shook the house, and I watched a picture of Joan on the wall shake. Uncle Jack opened his eyes and looked at me.

"I forgot how close the train was." He sat up. "Guess you ain't going to school."

I shook my head.

He leaned forward and looked me in the eye. "You were pretty brave last night," he whispered.

"Do the babies eat cereal?" Joan asked. She stood in the doorway with two bowls of Cheerios in her hands.

The babies liked cereal. When they were done eating, Cheerios were scattered everywhere. When we walked around the living room, we crushed them under our feet. The babies were twins. They were girls, Ruth and Rosemary. They both had their ears pierced and wore tiny diamond earrings. Their toenails were painted bright red. I couldn't tell them apart except that one of them cried a lot, and the other one was silent.

Joan spent the morning dressing them up in her clothes. She was the mommy, and they were her babies. Uncle Jack sat on the floor and ate Cheerios with us. We were watching cartoons when Alex Coolie dropped off some diapers.

"Hear anything?" Uncle Jack asked.

"Nothing. No one's seen him."

"He didn't just drop off the face of the earth."

"We aren't that lucky."

Alex sat down next to Jack and poured a bowl of cereal from the box that sat on the sky-blue coffee table. One of the babies had fallen asleep under it.

"He okay?" Alex asked as he poured milk over his Cheerios.

"It's a she."

"Oh," Alex said. "She okay?"

"Yeah, that one's the crier."

Alex ate his Cheerios. "I haven't had Cheerios in years. We used to have them all the time when we were kids."

Although there was a picture of Uncle Jack, a skinny kid with thick glasses, hanging on the wall, it was hard to imagine him doing normal kid stuff.

"Did you check up on the boys?" Uncle Jack asked.

"Yeah, Fizzy and Eddie are taking care of things. Those two wouldn't cheat you for the world. You know that."

"What about Vince? He working?"

"Looked like it. He was breaking a sweat."

"That don't mean a thing. Jail can get you out of shape pretty fast."

I sat on the couch. I still wore my clothes from the night before, and some of Amy's blood was smeared on my t-shirt. Amy moved through the living room picking up cereal from the floor, folding Joan's clothes, and looking out the window. She walked stiff, and I remembered the bruise on her side.

Joan and the other baby that wasn't asleep had built a tent by spreading a blanket over two kitchen chairs. They hid under it. I could hear Joan whispering.

"Sit down, Amy," Grandpa said. He walked into the living room with a cup of coffee in his hand. Cheerios crunched, and Joan and the baby giggled.

"I'm sorry about this mess. I'll clean it up. They're not usually this messy. It must be the excitement." Amy was talking fast, folding and unfolding one of Joan's dresses.

"Don't worry about that. *Good Housekeeping* ain't comin' over for a photo shoot."

Amy sat down uneasily in one of the green kitchen chairs. "George, I'm so sorry I drug all of you into this. I just didn't…"

"I don't want to hear anymore, okay? You're family and that's that."

"I ain't family anymore."

"No one gets out that easy," Uncle Jack said.

Amy smiled at him.

A car pulled up. Everyone got quiet. Joan crawled out from under the tent to watch. Uncle Jack stood up from the floor, and Alex sat his cereal bowl onto the coffee table. Amy walked over and picked up the sleeping baby.

I followed Uncle Jack into the hallway. A jump rope lay on the floor. I leaned against the dark wood paneling wall. Uncle Jack pulled back the yellow curtain on the door and looked outside.

"It's Samson," he said. I walked back into the living room. Amy had put the sleeping baby onto the couch. Joan sat on the other end of the couch chewing on a strand of her hair. Amy hadn't sat back down in the green chair, and I knew she hadn't relaxed. She still held her breath, fearful of my dad. I went to stand next to her.

My dad walked into the room with Vince Clayton. Vince Clayton didn't look much like Eddie. He had a white daddy. Vince had shaved his head, and now dark stubbles were appearing. Vince wore a heavy flannel shirt over a t-shirt, and he looked cold.

"Fall's coming in fast, George," he said to Grandpa.

"Does that every year, Vince. Boy, you look rough. Get in here and have some coffee; get something to eat. Where's Eddie?"

Vince stepped carefully into the living room. "He took Fizzy home. He'll be coming." Vince looked like a bird, tall and thin with a sharp nose. He looked around the room at one person then another.

My dad only looked at Uncle Jack. But I could tell he knew who was in the room.

"You get that job done over at the Courthouse?" Uncle Jack asked.

"Yeah, yeah. We got it done."

"You do it right?"

"Yes, Papa, we done it right."

"Smart ass." Uncle Jack grinned.

"I got bacon and eggs, Vince. How 'bout some bacon and eggs?" Grandpa offered.

"George, I don't want to put you out," Vince said.

"Nonsense, it's no trouble. You need to eat." Grandpa was already getting the eggs out of the refrigerator.

Vince sat down at the kitchen table and took off his flannel shirt. There were tattoos on his arms: a snake, a dragon, and a naked woman. My dad sat across from Vince next to Uncle Jack. Alex Coolie sat down next to Vince. I sat down beside my dad with my elbows resting on the cold yellow metal table. Cigarettes were passed between Vince and my dad. Lighters were exchanged. Joan brought a yellow ashtray from the living room. Ruth, who was the quiet baby, crawled onto my dad's lap. My dad didn't say anything, just smoked his cigarette while she played with his hair and his dark blue t-shirt. Amy stood behind me in the doorway that led to the hallway and the front door. She held Rosemary on her hip. There seemed to be no sound except the sound of bacon popping in the frying pan and Grandpa cracking eggs.

Uncle Jack lit a cigarette. "We need to decide what we're going to do."

"What can we do?" Vince asked. Grandpa slid a plate of food in front of him, and he ate it greedily, dipping bread into the yellow center of the eggs. "It seems to me we can't do anything until the bastard shows himself." His mouth was stuffed full. Alex Coolie looked at him with disgust. My dad was eating bacon and eggs, too, but he was eating them slowly.

"You can slow down, Vince. No one will take your food here," my dad said quietly.

Vince looked at my dad. His fork was frozen in midair just below his mouth. "Sorry, I'm not adjusted yet," he said. A look passed between my dad and Vince, and then Vince went back to eating, only slower this time.

"Well, he's likely to hide out for a while," Uncle Jack said. "There's never been a police report before. He's probably busy trying to keep his job." Coffee was poured and passed around. Grandpa sat down at the other end of the table. Ruth was bored with my dad. She climbed off his lap and disappeared into the living room. The little boy and girl came out of the clock. It was noon.

"More like convincing his cop buddies that it wasn't a big deal," Vince said.

"Well, I could miss work today because we only had that courthouse job, which is pretty routine, but I can't miss tomorrow," Uncle Jack said.

"Someone's got to be here with Amy and the babies," Alex said.

"I'm here," Grandpa said.

"Yeah, George but …"

"But hell," Grandpa was mad. "I can shoot a gun better than anyone of you."

This surprised me. How did Grandpa know how to shoot? I had never seen a gun in our house before. I thought of Uncle Jack's unloaded rifle.

"Dad, we don't want to shoot anyone if we don't have to," Uncle Jack said.

A look passed between my dad and Vince.

"Don't even think about it, Vince." My dad lit another cigarette. "It's that kind of thinking that will land you right back in jail."

"I just think that if we find him first…"

Uncle Jack interrupted him. "No, we are not cold-blooded killers. I can't go along with that."

"No one's talking about killing anyone," Vince said. He pushed his plate away from him and lit another cigarette. "I just think it would be easier if he just disappeared."

"You stupid motherfucker." My dad was angry, and I could feel Amy flinch behind me. "How old are you?"

"I'm 27."

"You're 27. You stupid son of a bitch, you want to spend the rest of your life in prison over some dumb fuck like Harvey Foster? I seen plenty of guys like you, all impulse, no brains. They keep coming back and coming back till finally they get life, and they got nowhere else to go. You got nowhere else to go, Vince?"

There was silence in the room. Joan had come to sit beside me. Outside, we heard a truck approach. Joan jumped up and ran to the window. "It's Eddie," she said.

Vince pushed his chair back. "What the hell is your problem, Sonny? You used to be the first person to defend someone in need. You'd be out hunting him down by now."

"I grew up," my dad muttered, crushing his cigarette into the ashtray.

"No." Vince stood up. Joan let Eddie into the house. "I think you lost your balls. What did prison do to you, man?"

"I grew up, Vince."

"No, you gave up. You're going to let that shit kick your family around. Let him scare you into hiding like rats waiting for him to show his face. Man, you ain't the Samson I remember."

My dad stood up. "What do you remember about me, Vince?"

"I remember that you never took any shit. God, Harrison and me, we worshipped you. You were like a god. No one fucked with you."

"Vince. I'm only three years older than you. You need to find better role models."

"Maybe you need to get some balls, man."

"Vince, sit down," Uncle Jack warned.

"No, I can't believe this. I mean we need to do something here. We need to find that motherfucker, and…"

"And what?" Uncle Jack asked.

My dad walked outside. Vince sat down and lit another cigarette. His hands shook.

Uncle Jack followed my dad outside, and I followed Uncle Jack. My dad stood beside Uncle Jack's truck. I stood on the porch and watched as Uncle Jack approached my dad.

"What the hell's the matter with him?" my dad shouted. "He's going to get himself killed just like Harrison. I ain't going back to prison. I ain't going back to save his ass or defend hers. I just ain't going back." My dad rested his arms on the bed of the truck and bent over to lean his head against the side of the truck. "Doesn't he know that's what I want to do? Doesn't he know I want to rip that motherfucker apart? You just don't beat on women. You just don't."

I moved into the yard and stood a few feet away from them.

My dad's voice got lower. "When I saw her, it took everything I had not to kill that motherfucker. What am I supposed to do, Jack? What am I supposed to do?"

"We need to keep cool heads here. I think it's best if we take Amy and the girls to Alex's to stay awhile. You can't keep cool around her."

"What the hell does that mean?"

"Come on, Samson. There's a lot of baggage there."

"You think I want her back?" My dad said. "What the fuck is wrong with you? Don't you know that every time I look at her I see everything we did to Lou? Everything I did to Lou. She trusted me."

My dad stopped talking.

The sun shone brightly. Some of the leaves on the maple tree were turning yellow. Everything was silent, and I felt scared of the silence.

My dad straightened himself. "I didn't do right by her, Jack. I didn't do right by either one of them."

Uncle Jack patted my dad's arm. "Well, now maybe, this is your chance to get it right."

There was a sharp pain in my stomach. My dad had cheated on Lou with Amy. My dad turned and looked in my direction, but he didn't look at me.

"Maybe it's too late," he said to Uncle Jack.

CHAPTER 15

Alex Coolie lived right on Main Street in Johnstown in a big house that had three bedrooms and a big black piano that filled the living room. He also had a black cat named Chicken who only came out from under the couch at night. He was afraid of everyone but Alex and Joan. He didn't even like Uncle Jack, and he lived there now.

Amy, Rosemary, and Ruth slept upstairs in one of the bedrooms. Grandpa had his own room, too, but I couldn't hear him breathing because he was too far away, and it was always noisy in Johnstown. Cars were always driving by, and the people in the houses across the street were always having a party or fighting.

Chicken slept with Joan and me in the living room. Alex gave us some old sleeping bags that he had in his attic, and sometimes, Joan and me pretended that we were camping. We slept under the window next to the piano. I reached up and played with the curtain. It was soft and white in the light from the street.

"Get the fuck out," a woman's voice from across the street screeched.

"Believe me. I'm going," was the man's reply.

Joan slept right through it. Nothing bothered her. Chicken was asleep on her chest, and he rose every time she breathed. In the dark, it looked like he was floating.

"I know you've been with her," the woman screamed louder.

I missed my own bed and the trains. And I wanted things to be the way they were before, before my dad, before Amy, and I wanted to be able to hear

Grandpa breathing.

"Oh, come on, baby. You know that didn't mean a thing," the man pleaded. I wondered if my dad had said this to my mom about Amy.

It was too dark to see Joan's fingernails, but I know they were bright pink. Every night before bed, Amy and her painted them.

Amy said, "A woman always looks put together if her fingernails are painted." Or something like that. Amy's bruises were fading to that yellow-green color bruises always got after a while.

"I'm not putting up with this no more," the woman screamed.

Chicken jumped up and ran away. I looked around the room for him. Headlights moved across the wall as someone pulled along the curb across the street. Chicken was hiding under the piano.

"Come on, baby. I'm sorry. I won't do it again." The man was begging now.

"Will you two shut up." This was another man's voice. "Some people have to work in the morning."

"Mind your own business," the first man screamed back.

I let go of the curtain and rolled over. "Come on, Chicken," I whispered. "It's only the crazy neighbors."

I reached out my hand.

Everything exploded behind me. Window glass flew everywhere. The curtains and curtain rod fell down on my head, and tears came to my eyes. There were more explosions. One hit the piano, and it banged in the darkness. I heard Chicken hissing. Then, Joan screamed.

The light came on. I looked at my arm. There was a big piece of glass sticking out of it. I felt cold air on my back where the window used to be. Uncle Jack and Alex were there. Alex had a gun in his hand, and Uncle Jack was in his underwear.

"I'll call the cops," Alex said.

Joan wouldn't stop screaming. Uncle Jack bent down and gently lifted my arm, so Joan could crawl out from under me and run away. I heard her crying, and Grandpa talking to her. But I couldn't move because of the glass in my arm and the curtain and curtain rod on top of me. Uncle Jack took them off of me.

"Where's Chicken?" I asked. Uncle Jack was checking to see if I was hurt anywhere else. I thought my head was bleeding because it felt wet. I was trying to touch my forehead with the arm that didn't have the glass in it when Uncle

Jack yelled at me to keep still.

"Whoa, man, you must have really pissed someone off."

It was the guy from next door who was fighting with his wife or girlfriend before. I couldn't see him, but I knew he was looking in through the broken window.

"Get the hell out of here," Uncle Jack growled.

I got to ride in the ambulance with the piece of glass still in my arm. The ambulance lady kept trying to talk to me about school and my favorite TV show, but I was more interested in the way I could look through the glass in my arm like looking through a window.

"Twelve-year-old female. Someone shot up her house. Large piece of glass in her arm," the ambulance driver said to someone on the other end of the radio.

I heard my name, and that's all I remembered until I woke up in the hospital the next day. It was not the same hospital that we went to with Amy. Everything in this room seemed cleaner. These walls were light blue with animals on them. I was probably in the children's ward, I thought, and this made me mad. I wasn't a little kid anymore. It was my 13th birthday. My arm was wrapped in a big white bandage. My head had a small Band-Aid on it, so the curtain rod must not have hurt me too bad. I felt kind of weird like everything was foggy. I looked through the crack in the curtain that separated my bed from other beds. Grandpa stood there. He wore a pair of red pants and a navy-blue shirt. He was talking to a man I didn't recognize.

Uncle Jack walked through the curtain and stood next to the bed, blocking my view.

"Hey, Helen," he said.

"Who is Grandpa talking to?"

"Just another cop. It's his job to make sure everything's okay."

"Is everything okay?" I figured this was finally it. They would take us away for sure now. Sleeping in sleeping bags, being shot at, I figured people wouldn't think that was a good way for a kid to be living.

"Sure, everything's okay," Uncle Jack said as he sat on the bed next to me. He leaned over and whispered, "No one's getting sent away."

I was happy about that. "Is Joan okay? What about Chicken? Did the Sheriff shoot at us?"

Uncle Jack laughed. "How much of that stuff did they give you?" He was talking about the drugs that was coming into my arm and making my head foggy.

I didn't laugh.

"Joan's scared but fine. We don't know who shot at us."

"But it was probably the sheriff," I said.

Uncle Jack shrugged. "I'd put him as the number one suspect but not the only one."

I was confused.

"Johnstown can be pretty rough sometimes. Might not have been about us at all."

"If it's so bad, why do you live there?"

Uncle Jack smiled. "For the most part, Alex and I are not bothered by anyone."

I thought about this for a moment. "Because you're…" I paused. "Mr. Coolie says I shouldn't say queer."

"Probably not." Uncle Jack smiled.

"What should I say?"

"We are your uncles." He laughed.

I smiled.

"What about Chicken?" I asked.

"He's at the vet. He'll be all right."

Uncle Jack smiled at me. "By the way, Happy Birthday. Hell of a way to celebrate though."

I nodded.

CHAPTER 16

CHICKEN AND ME SAT AT THE TOP OF THE BASEMENT STAIRS AT FIZZY'S HOUSE listening to Amy and her mother talk. They sat at the kitchen table drinking coffee. I didn't like Amy's mom. She didn't look anything like Amy. She was big and tall with bright white hair, and when she talked, her voice was rough.

My arm was still bandaged. I couldn't wait to go to school again to scare everyone with my scar especially, Mark and Mitchell Maxwell. It would gross them out for sure. The stub that used to be Chicken's back leg was still in a bandage, too. Chicken liked me now. I carried him around a lot because it's hard for a cat to walk with only three legs.

"Listen, he's your husband," Amy's mother said.

"I know," Amy said. Her voice seemed so quiet compared to her mother's.

It was a warm day, and I could hear Joan, Ruth, and Rosemary through the open kitchen window. They were out in the backyard with Fizzy and Eddie Clayton. I could hear them taking turns making Eddie push them in the tire swing that hung in the backyard.

"You got to do the right thing," her mother said.

"I know, but I just can't. You don't understand."

"What's keeping you here? Samson?"

"No, not Samson. God no, that's over. You know Samson never loved me. It was always about Lou."

"I told you that then. Remember? He just wanted the milk without buying the cow. You'd have been a whore with a bastard child if she hadn't have died.

Luckily for you."

Amy shifted her bare feet under the table. The sun reflected off the green linoleum of the kitchen floor. Amy's toenails were painted bright blue.

"You got to do the right thing. You got a nice house. You want to give that up for a shack like this? Harvey's a good man."

"He beat me," Amy said softly.

"All men get a little crazy jealous sometimes. You don't go running off. You take the good with the bad."

Joan ran into the kitchen and opened the refrigerator door.

"What are you getting, Joan?" Amy asked.

"We want Pepsi," Joan said. The refrigerator door slammed shut, and she walked back outside.

"Listen," Amy's mother said. "I talked to him."

"Mother," Amy said. "That's how he knew we were at Alex's."

"We don't know that he shot at you. I mean Alex does live in that rough neighborhood. And Harvey swore to me it was not him. He's awfully sorry."

"I don't know if I can leave Joan again," Amy said.

"Joan is fine with George. And you can't save her now. That's water under the bridge. Ruth and Rosemary will have a good, decent life. They won't grow up to be like the oldest one. What's her name? Helen. Just like her daddy. She'll be in prison, too."

I felt embarrassed by the way Amy's mother talked about me. Chicken rubbed his head against my bandage.

"Helen is fine. She's a good girl."

"She punched you in the mouth. She should have had a belt on her butt for that one."

There was a pause.

"That was my fault," Amy said.

Her mother made a grunting noise. "All I'm asking is that you talk to Harvey. If you don't like what he says, you can go right back to this trash," Amy's mother said.

I heard her stand up and leave, slamming the door behind her.

I heard Amy sigh, and I knew she would go back to the sheriff. I didn't understand why, but I knew it was true because I felt this dull ache in the pit of my stomach. I didn't care because I knew grownups left you. That's what they do. I had been a stupid kid about my dad's return. I had expected some great TV dad, but all I got was another screwed up adult. I knew not to hope anymore, but Joan hadn't learned that yet.

For a second, I wondered if I could convince Amy to stay with us if I just said the right thing, but I knew that was stupid kid thinking. With the sheriff, she had a nice house and a man that said he loved her. With us, she got nothing except my dad's anger and guilt.

The next morning, Amy and the babies were gone, and Joan sobbed.

"Dry your eyes, Joan," Grandpa said, wiping her face with the end of his bright pink shirt. "We can head on home now."

I never shed a tear. I was angry, and I swore if I ever saw Amy again I'd hit her, only harder this time.

CHAPTER 17

I sat on the porch swing in a big flannel coat that I had found in Grandpa's closet. It was red plaid with black lining. It was so big that the bottom of it covered my knees, and the sleeves hid my hands. Even though it was cold enough to see my breath, I was warm except for my face. I was swinging the porch swing so high that it was hitting the side of the house.

"You're going to leave a dent in your Grandpa's house," Vince said as he stepped out onto the porch. He sat on the porch steps and lit a cigarette.

"What's eating you?" he asked.

I shrugged.

"Amy's leaving piss you off?" he asked.

"She's not my mom. Why should I care?"

"Oh, so you know about Lou."

"What do you know about it?"

"I knew Lou. Hell, I practically lived here growing up. My mom had rotten taste in men."

I looked out into the yard. It was bare and brown.

"After Eddie's dad disappeared, my mom got a new boyfriend. He was a mean drunk. He was a truck driver, so he was only around on the weekends. At first, Eddie and me would just take off when he got mean. One night, we walked barefoot in the snow to get here. After a while, we'd call your Grandpa to come and get us. Then after that, we just showed up on Friday night and stayed all weekend." He stopped talking and looked at me. I looked back at him, and he looked away.

"Anyhow, I knew Lou. God, I was half in love with her. Everyone was. She was amazing, beautiful and tough. Your dad never showed you a picture of her?"

I shook my head.

"Wow, he should. You know Lou could have been a model or something. I can't believe you've never seen a picture of her."

I tried to picture this beautiful mom of mine, but I couldn't. Just my luck, I thought. I got a beautiful mother, and I'm born looking like my dad.

"She was great."

Vince smoked his cigarette, and I slowed down the swing.

"You know I'd have killed Harvey if that was what your family wanted."

I stopped swinging. "You'd go to jail."

Vince laughed. "I'm heading for life anyway. I'd rather do it for a good reason."

"You like prison?"

Vince laughed again. "I'm used to it."

I started swinging again. "My dad's right. You're stupid."

He laughed. "That's probably true." He tossed his cigarette into the yard. "But I'd have done it for your family. Eddie, too. He'd take care of your family. And that goes for you and your sister. You ever need us to handle anything, we'll do it."

I stopped the swing, and I thought about this.

"I don't need you to handle anything for me. I can take care of myself."

He stood up. "Well, the offer stands," he said and went back inside.

I looked out into the brown, bare yard. Eddie Clayton stood leaning against Uncle Jack's truck.

He nodded at me, and I knew he had heard what Vince said to me.

CHAPTER 18

Joan stood guard while I searched my dad's room for the box of photo-graphs.

"I don't like this," Joan whispered. "Grandpa said we were supposed to stay out of Daddy's room."

"Just shut up and keep watch. I told you. I'll take the blame." I stood on a chair and looked through some boxes on a shelf.

"I don't understand. What are you looking for?"

"Pictures of my mom."

"Pictures of mom?"

"I'll explain it later."

Joan looked confused.

Although our grandmother had blurted it out, I hadn't talked to Joan about my mom and our dad, and she never asked me either. She still called our dad "daddy", so I didn't want her to know the truth about my dad's guilt, but I thought it would be better coming from me because sooner or later she'd find out anyway, even if she didn't want to know. Nothing stays a secret forever.

I couldn't find the pictures on the shelf. I got off the chair and went to look under the bed. I pulled out a box and opened the lid. On top of the box lay a black gun. I picked it up and showed it to Joan. Now, we knew why our dad didn't want us in his room. How long had he had this gun? Why did he have it? I thought I knew the answer to that, and it made my hands shake.

"Put it down, Helen," Joan begged.

I lay it on the bed.

I searched through the box. It was filled with photo albums, newspaper clippings, and loose pictures. Joan ran over. She kneeled down to look into the box.

"Now what?"

"We have to take it somewhere where we can look at it and not get caught."

"Where?"

We were both thinking hard. "Let's just take it to our room for now. Sonny's with Uncle Jack. He won't be back for a while."

I refused to call him "dad" or "daddy".

I pulled the box across the hall into our room and dumped the box onto the bed. Pictures fell everywhere. We gathered them all onto the bed and started looking at them. Some were just dumb school pictures of us or pictures of us with Grandma. One must have been at Easter because we were all dressed in matching yellow dresses. We all looked unhappy.

There was a wedding picture. It was my dad and a woman I didn't recognize. I turned the picture over. Sonny and Lou, August 1, 1963. My mom and dad's wedding. I was born November 4, 1963, so my mom was already pregnant with me, but you couldn't really tell it in this picture. My mom was beautiful. She was the opposite of Amy: tall with dark eyes and dark hair. She wore a light purple dress, and she was holding a bouquet of purple flowers. In another picture, she looked tough in jeans and a black t-shirt. A cigarette hung from the corner of her mouth. There was a picture of her holding a red wrinkly baby. I flipped the picture over Lou and Helen. The red wrinkly baby was me.

There were pictures of my mom and pictures of the red wrinkly baby being held by everyone: Helen Coolie, Alex Coolie, Mr. Coolie, my dad, Uncle Jack, Grandma and even Uncle Harrison. He was a skinny teenager in this picture, maybe a little older than I was. I stared at his face, trying to remember him, but I couldn't.

"Look," Joan said. She handed me a newspaper clipping. It was my mother's obituary. Her death was listed as a railroad accident. She died September 1, 1964. Joan was born February 14, 1965. I did the math in my head. Amy was already pregnant with Joan when my mom died. My dad had cheated on Amy, and here was the proof although I already knew it. I sat down on the bed.

Joan sat next to me. "So, Daddy was married to your mom before he married mine?"

I nodded.

"If we have different moms, are we still sisters?"

I'd thought about this. "I think we're half-sisters."

She was quiet. "I want to still be your full sister," Joan said. She was sitting next to me, so she gave me a sideways hug.

I patted her arm with my hand. I noticed my ugly, red scar. Vince said when I grew up I could get a tattoo there of a snake, and I'd have the meanest tattoo ever and no one would mess with me, only he said the "f" word. I liked the idea of no one messing with me.

"We're sisters," I said, and I meant it.

"Where are the wedding pictures of daddy and my mom?" Leave it to Joan to want to see the wedding pictures. She was always playing wedding, dressing and undressing Barbie and Ken a thousand times. She was always talking about her wedding, what dress she would wear and what flowers she'd have. Sometimes, it drove me crazy.

We started digging through the pictures and were about to give up when we found a wedding picture of my dad and Amy. She wore a white dress and was clearly pregnant. My dad wore a suit that didn't quite fit him. The sleeves were too short. They stood in front of a courthouse.

Joan was disappointed. I guess she expected a big fairytale wedding, not this one sorry picture. She took the picture over to a corner where her dolls were and didn't say anything.

I started to put the photos back into the box. I kept the one where my mom looked tough. I recognized my Grandma's handwriting on the front of a photo album. She had written a Bible quote. "Eye for eye, tooth for tooth, hand for hand, foot for foot. Burning for Burning, wound for wound, stripe for stripe. Exodus 21:24."

I opened the album. It was filled with newspaper clippings about my dad getting arrested and Uncle Harrison's death.

"I will be an enemy unto thine enemies, and an adversary unto thine adversaries. Exodus 23:22." My grandmother had written over a picture of my dad in handcuffs.

The headline said, "Car theft ring stopped by local sheriff." I read the article. It said the sheriff went to arrest Uncle Harrison and my dad. Uncle Harrison attacked and shot the sheriff, and the sheriff shot him in self-defense. I read it again. It said nothing about my dad getting shot. And how had the sheriff arrested my dad if he'd been shot? I wasn't even sure the sheriff could stop my dad when he wasn't hurt. The sheriff was tall, but my dad was a lot bigger than him.

Now, I knew why my grandma didn't believe it. I still wasn't convinced that my dad killed Uncle Harrison like my grandma was, but I was convinced this story wasn't the truth.

I kept the newspaper story. I searched for an obituary for Uncle Harrison, but there didn't seem to be one. I bet Grandma kept it.

I heard a car. Joan looked at me frightened. I knew by the look on her face that she was worried about my dad finding out that we had seen the gun.

I shoved all the pictures in the box and carried it into my dad's room. I closed the lid before I slid it back under my dad's bed. I put the gun on top the box, just like I found it.

CHAPTER 19

Miss Mason was writing math problems on the chalkboard, and I wasn't paying attention. I was thinking about my dad and the sheriff and the gun and what happened to Uncle Harrison. I was trying to think of a way to find out the truth.

There was a clock over the chalkboard. It was an ugly green clock that sort of looked like a flower, and it ticked loudly. I hated that clock.

It was close to Thanksgiving, so there were paper turkeys hanging from the ceiling. They were made of construction paper stuffed with newspaper strips with glued on feathers and eyes. No one's turkey ever looked like Miss Mason's. Someone's eyes were always missing. Feathers fell off, and some turkeys were so fat they were ripping, and others didn't have enough stuffing. And Timmy Gilbert always ate the glue before Miss Mason could take it away from him. Most of us thought we were too old to be making construction paper turkeys, but Miss Mason loved art projects, and she always acted like ours were the greatest things she'd ever seen. No one wanted to disappoint her.

It was almost eleven o'clock. The train would be coming soon. The train passed by the school every day at eleven o'clock, rattling the windows. The teachers had learned to plan around it and be patient while we watched it pass. None of us thought we were too old to get out of our seats and watch the train pass. Uncle Jack said the school board talked about putting up a fence. He knew this because he was on the school board because no one else wanted to be after Mrs. Houseman died, and they needed twelve people or else they couldn't get state funding.

My stomach was growling. I'd only eaten half my cereal. Mark Maxwell sat in front of me. He was throwing little spitballs into Timmy Gilbert's hair. Timmy wore a sweater with a train knitted on it. I bet his mom knitted it for him.

Mitchell Maxwell was sitting in the corner. He was in trouble again and had to think about what he'd done. I could tell Mitch wasn't thinking about anything. He was just kicking the floor with the heel of his boot, and it made an annoying thumping sound.

I started to get a little crazy with that chalk moving across the board and the thumping of that boot and the white balls landing in Timmy's hair and that clock ticking and ticking. Plus, I was dying of hunger. When the eleven o'clock train started coming, the kids jumped out of their seats to go to the window to watch it pass.

Only I didn't move because I watched a pen on Miss Mason's desk shake, fall to the floor, and roll away. The turkeys over our heads shook, and a string holding one of them broke, and the turkey came apart as it fell down, and newspaper strips floated to the floor.

Then, the screeching started. It was like a thousand fingernails scraping across the chalkboard. Miss Mason dropped her chalk, and some kids screamed and covered their ears. I got up and ran to the window. The train seemed to be bouncing across the track like a Slinky.

"The train is wrecking," Mark Maxwell shouted. But I could hardly hear him because everything was so loud. The train tipped over and skidded, knocking over everything on the playground. Swings flew through the air.

Miss Mason started pulling kids away from the window and pushing them toward the door. Some kids hid under their desks. Mark Maxwell had already run out into the hall, and Mitch was crawling slowly past Miss Mason's desk. One of the boxcars was sliding on its side right toward our classroom. It hit the side of the building, and all the windows broke, and glass flew through the air. I was knocked down. Miss Mason was on the floor next to me, covering Timmy Gilbert with her body.

The noises outside stopped. The only thing you could hear was kids crying. Miss Mason stood up. Her dress was dirty, and there were little pieces of glass in her hair. It looked like snow. A part of the red boxcar stuck through the wall. Miss Mason made sure we were okay and got us all into the hallway. Mitch Maxwell was crying, and Timmy hadn't let go of Miss Mason's hand since she had picked him up off the floor.

We walked outside. It was cold, and none of us had jackets.

"That was way cool," Mark Maxwell said, jumping up and down to keep warm.

I was about to agree until Miss Mason hushed him.

The principal walked around broken pieces of the train to talk to each of the teachers and get a head count. It was decided that every class should go and wait in a local business until parents came or transportation could be arranged. Some classes went to Woolworth's five and dime store, some waited at the bank, a few at Holmes' Insurance. Our class was supposed to wait at the Sapphire Restaurant and Bar. Miss Mason protested this as she shook glass from her hair. But there was no choice. There weren't that many businesses in town, and the train blocked most of the street. Miss Mason made us hold hands as we crossed what used to be the playground. The sliding board was jammed into the cafeteria wall. We stopped to look at it before we walked down the street. Police, ambulance, and fire trucks were parked everywhere.

"Cool," Mark Maxwell whispered.

Miss Mason opened the door of the Sapphire Bar, and we walked in. It was very dark in there except for the string of Christmas lights that twinkled over the bar. Once my eyes had adjusted, I saw Fizzy sitting at the bar and Vince standing behind the bar.

We all stood close together by the door. There was a pool table and a jukebox in one corner next to a dance floor.

"Wow," Mark whispered.

"Come on, kids," Vince said. "Have a seat." He pointed to a group of tables that surrounded the dance floor. He walked toward us, smiling. He winked at me, and everyone looked at me.

Miss Mason was very nervous. "I'm sure the principal spoke to you about us waiting here until…"

She paused as a big drunk man wandered out of the bathroom. She was obviously very frightened.

"Sit down," Vince said again.

The big man nodded toward us then walked over to sit on his bar stool.

Miss Mason inched her way toward the table. We followed her; none of us were letting go of each other's hands. The Sapphire Bar was the meanest bar in town. Everyone knew not to go near there. People were always fighting.

We all sat down at the tables. The chairs were red vinyl with metal legs. The tables were silver metal. Little black ashtrays sat on the tables.

"Listen, why don't I get you kids some cheeseburgers and fries?" Vince offered.

Some kids were excited, but others were afraid. No one knew whether or not to eat the food there.

"Can we have cokes, Vince?" I asked.

He looked at Miss Mason, and she nodded.

"Sure, Helen. Cokes, too."

He walked away to get started on the food, and Fizzy walked over to the table.

"Hey Sugarplum," he said to me. "You make that train wreck?"

I shook my head. I knew I was supposed to be embarrassed because I knew Vince and Fizzy, but I wasn't. Besides, it impressed everyone in my class. They thought I was tough, some kind of outlaw or something.

Fizzy sat down next to Miss Mason who looked like she might faint. "So, who's going to tell me what happened?"

Everyone started talking at once.

After we ate and talked to Fizzy, Vince offered to play the jukebox, so we could dance. Everyone thought this was a great idea.

"Let me show you how to do the hustle," Vince offered. He was talking to us but looking at Miss Mason, and Miss Mason blushed.

We all wanted to learn it. Vince lined us up and showed us the steps. Even Miss Mason danced with us. She tried to get Timmy Gilbert to dance, but he wouldn't.

"God don't like dancing," he said.

All the kids looked at each other.

"Your church don't allow it," Vince said. "That's cool. I can respect that."

"Oh, go on boy," the big man from the bar shouted. "God ain't watching."

"Larry," Vince said.

"I've been sitting on this bar stool since I was his age, and I ain't never seen God in here once."

"Yeah, it's too dark for God to see in here," Mark Maxwell said.

"Ain't seen any of your church folks in here either," Larry mumbled.

This seemed to almost convince Timmy. He stepped onto the dance floor. "I don't know," Timmy said.

"Don't do anything you're not comfortable with," Miss Mason said.

"Go on now, boy. Come Sunday you can get God's forgiveness," Larry said.

This convinced Timmy. Vince played another song, and we all danced except for the kids who were spinning around on the bar stools.

We were trying to do the hustle when the door opened, and a group of parents walked in. Everyone froze.

"Well, I'll be damned. I never expected to see the good church folks in here," Larry said, lifting his beer to them.

"What are you doing?!" Mrs. Gilbert screamed. She was a thin woman with long bony fingers that she used to grab Timmy's wrist. "We don't dance."

"But Mom…"

She smacked Timmy's butt in front of all of us.

Vince turned off the jukebox, and we all got quiet.

Mark Maxwell was spinning on one of the bar stools. "I don't feel so good," he said. He leaned forward and threw up.

"This is all your fault!" One of the mothers screeched at Miss Mason. "How could you bring children into a place like this?!"

"It was the only place left," Miss Mason whispered. "I was told I had to."

Parents grabbed their children and shoved them toward the door.

"We will have a meeting about this," they muttered.

"Letting children in a bar."

"Did you see her dancing with that…?"

"I thought he was still in jail."

The door closed, and I was the only one left with Miss Mason and Vince.

"I need a drink," Miss Mason muttered.

Vince laughed, and she smiled at him.

I sat down next to Miss Mason and waited for someone to come for me.

We waited for about 30 minutes, and then the door opened, and my grandmother walked in. I froze. My grandmother was dressed in a too short, purple, paisley dress, a purple coat, and a pair of high-heeled boots. Everything about her outfit was pretty, but somehow Grandma always looked scary. Maybe it was the way she charged into a room, daring anyone to stand up to her.

"Mrs. Cooper," Miss Mason said. "I wasn't expecting you."

My grandmother stared her down like a cat about to eat a mouse. "I am Helen's legal guardian."

Technically, she probably was, somewhere on some school paperwork, but I knew this appearance had nothing to do with me or my safety.

I looked at Miss Mason, Vince, Fizzy, and I even looked at Larry who I didn't know, but I knew there was nothing they could do. They could not help me. I sighed. A kid always had to do what adults told them to, and I hated it.

I stood up. "Vince, make sure my grandpa and Uncle Jack know where I am."

My grandmother laughed. It was a horrible sound. "Don't be dramatic, Helen. I'm just taking you home."

We stepped outside; the sun was bright. Pieces of the train were scattered all around the school. The monkey bars were lying upside down in the middle of Main Street.

I looked at my grandmother. "So, why are you here?"

She clicked her tongue. "So suspicious. Come on, my car's down this way."

I didn't move.

"Helen, come on." She was angry.

"Why are you here?"

My grandmother stomped her high heeled boot. "You are so much like your dad. I could shake you, you little brat."

I stared her down.

"All right, I was in town. I heard about the train, and I thought this would be the only time I could get you alone."

"Why do you want me alone?"

For a second, there was a flicker of fear in my stomach, but then I smiled. No matter how mean she was, I knew I could be meaner. I could beat her in a fight.

"I know with your dad coming home you have this great idea that he's some kind of hero."

I wanted to laugh. Not anymore. That was Joan, I thought.

"Well, he's not a hero. He's dangerous, a murderer. It's not safe for him to be in your house with you and your sister."

I remembered the gun. This was the first time I had thought about the possibility that he was dangerous to me or my family. It always seemed like he was a danger to others, not us.

"If you're so worried, why don't you talk to Grandpa?"

She was angry again. "I tried to tell that old fool, but Samson and him always did have a bond."

"You mean he liked my dad best, just like you liked Uncle Harrison the best."

I felt sorry for Uncle Jack. Who loved him best?

"You don't understand. You won't, not until you have children of your own. Harrison was my baby." She actually sounded like she was going to cry. "I thought there wouldn't be any other babies for me, all I'd have was stubborn, disrespectful Samson and Jackson."

"What was wrong with Uncle Jack?"

She snorted. "What was I supposed to do with him? Share my clothes with him? Let him parade around town like that?"

"Like what?"

"You know he's different. He's not natural."

"I like Uncle Jack," I said.

"How are you ever going to be raised right in that house? I just don't know. I just thought if you knew who your dad truly was…"

"I'd be on your side," I interrupted her.

"You'd be safe."

"I read the newspaper article. It didn't say my dad murdered Uncle Harrison. Why do you think he did? Just because you don't like him."

"I know he did. He was mean and on dope. Always was jealous of Harrison. And he's guilty. You can see that guilty look in his black eyes."

I realized my grandmother was guilty, too. That no matter how much make-up she wore, she couldn't hide her shame. I had never noticed it before. Maybe it was the harsh sunlight that made it obvious or maybe it was because I knew how she felt. Every time, the Maxwell's told anyone about my dad, every time, I find out something new about my family, I felt ashamed, and shame was like a thick coating on your skin, and you never felt clean.

"What did you do?" I asked. "What do you feel guilty about?"

She looked startled.

"My God, Helen, we've been looking everywhere for you." Uncle Jack came running toward me. Joan ran after him, and my dad walked behind her.

Joan hugged me. "It was so cool. We got candy in the five and dime. Where were you?"

"I was in there," I said, pointing toward the Sapphire Bar.

"Wow," Joan said.

"What are you doing here?" my dad asked my grandmother.

"I was in town, and I heard about the accident. I am still Helen's legal guardian."

Uncle Jack looked surprised.

My dad and grandma stared at each other for a moment, and my grandma walked away, being careful not to step on the firehoses that looked like white snakes slithering down the street. I was surprised that she walked away so easily.

"Come on, I got the truck parked around the corner," Uncle Jack said.

"Where's Grandpa?" I asked as we walked toward the truck.

"The car wouldn't start, so he couldn't come to get you," my dad said.

As we turned the corner, we found ourselves face-to-face with the sheriff. He was dressed in his uniform, trying to look important and involved, but it was clear he had no idea what to do.

When he saw my dad, he grinned. "Well, well, Samson, it looks like I got my wife back. I told you she knows when she's got it good."

My dad's fists clenched, but the look on his face didn't change.

"Samson, let's just go," Uncle Jack said.

My dad nodded, and the sheriff laughed.

"Harvey, it's best to let it be," Uncle Jack warned.

"Let it be. You all are the ones who need to stay out of our business. We were fine until he came back into town. She's my wife. I can do what I want with her. She'll always come back to me."

"Harvey," Uncle Jack said in his preacher voice, "we don't want anything to do with you and Amy. That's between you and her, but you shouldn't be hitting a woman."

Harvey laughed, but it wasn't a real laugh. It was mean. "I don't think a queer preacher's got any business telling me how to handle a woman." Harvey reached into his pocket and pulled out a pack of cigarettes; he lit one. "He give that little 'how to treat a woman' sermon to Harrison?" He was looking at my dad.

Every muscle in my dad's body was tense. I could feel the heat coming off of him. He seemed like a wild animal about to attack.

"What's he talking about?' Uncle Jack asked.

"Nothing. He's not talking about anything." It was a clear warning.

"Good, that sermon wouldn't have worked with him either." He flicked ashes to the ground. "Some women just drive a man to hit them. You just can't be good to some women. They have it coming."

When my dad finally exploded, I expected it to be loud like the train wrecking, but it was quiet. My dad reached out and grabbed the sheriff by the shirt and slammed him against the wall of a nearby building exactly like I had done to Mark Maxwell. I wondered if my dad saw red, too.

Joan screamed, and Uncle Jack tried to move to stop it, but it happened so quickly that he couldn't.

"You need to shut the fuck up," my dad whispered.

The sheriff was stunned, and all his big talk was gone. He looked like a deflated balloon. He looked scared.

"Any man that hits a woman is a coward who needs his ass kicked," my dad said.

"That include Harrison?" the sheriff said.

I looked at Uncle Jack. It was clear from his facial expression that he didn't know what woman Uncle Harrison had hit.

"We agreed to keep our mouths shut. Let's not start talking now."

The sheriff didn't say anything.

My dad slammed him hard against the wall again. "And I know it was you that shot up Alex's house. Leave my family alone." I never heard someone so angry speak so softly. His voice was a deep whisper like it came from the bottom of a well.

"I did not. I absolutely did not," the sheriff said. "I didn't even know she was there until Helen got hurt. That wasn't me. Maybe you got other enemies."

"Samson, let's go," Uncle Jack said again.

My dad didn't move.

"Daddy," Joan said.

My dad looked at her, and then he released the sheriff. My dad moved away from him, and Joan reached out to take my dad's hand. He took it, and we walked to Uncle Jack's truck. My dad helped Joan and me into the back, and then he got into the front of the truck with Uncle Jack.

As we drove away, I heard Uncle Jack ask my dad about Uncle Harrison and what woman he hit.

"It's in the past, Jack," my dad said. "All that was left on the mountain, and it needs to stay there."

But I knew neither Uncle Jack nor I was going to be satisfied with that answer.

CHAPTER 20

Uncle Jack took me to a meeting about the train wreck. It was in the basement of Uncle Jack's church. To get to the basement, we had to walk down some narrow spiraled wooden stairs. In the gray, cold basement, rows of folding chairs were set up to face a long table covered with a purple tablecloth. A picture of Jesus hung behind the table. Jesus was kneeling, looking up to heaven. Some ladies from the church were making coffee in big silver containers. Uncle Jack shook hands with the principal and some other men I didn't know.

"If we could please get started," a man in a brown suit announced.

I sat on one of the folding chairs at the back of the room. Vince and Eddie Clayton leaned against the wall, next to me. Everyone started coming into the room and taking seats in the brown metal chairs marked "FCC" for the First Church of Christ. Uncle Jack sat at the purple table. The man in the brown suit was the school board president. He introduced himself and everyone else. His name was Walter Holmes from Holmes Insurance Company. Uncle Jack wore a black suit with a blue tie. Reverend Paine sat in the front row. He was the Sunday preacher at Uncle Jack's church. His hair looked like someone had sprayed fake snow on his head, and he used an oxygen mask to breathe. A little green oxygen tank with wheels sat on the floor next to him. Timmy Gilbert's mother sat in front of me. She wore a peach skirt, a white sweater, and carried a big peach purse. Timmy's father sat next to her. He was a short man who wore a pair of blue Dickey pants and a red sweater with a train knitted on it. Timmy's mom had one leg crossed over the other and was swinging her foot back and forth rapidly.

Miss Mason walked into the room. Her hair was pulled back into a pony-tail, and she wore a black dress and a pair of black heels. She sat down a few rows behind Mr. and Mrs. Gilbert. I heard Timmy's mom grunt.

"All right, I think we should get started. The kids have been out of school now for about a week and half, and the railroad officials tell us it will take some time to clean up," Mr. Holmes said.

"How much time?" someone from the back shouted. I turned around. Some people stood against the back wall. They were mostly men.

Mr. Holmes pointed to three men sitting in the front row. "These gentlemen are here from the railroad. They can answer that question better than I can."

The men nodded. One of them stood up. "We estimate anywhere from three to six weeks."

There was mumbling.

"That's a long time."

"What are we going to do with the kids until then?"

"Meyersdale for sure."

"All right, all right," Mr. Holmes said. "So, there we have it. Now, we have to make some decisions. You know the county has wanted us to bus our kids over to Meyersdale for years. I'm not interested in that any more than you are. Garrett students should go to the Garrett school. So, thanks to a generous offer from Reverend Paine and Reverend Cooper, this church is open to our students until the school is repaired."

"Can all our kids fit into the church?" someone else from the back asked.

I turned around.

"If we use the basement and all the Sunday school rooms," Uncle Jack said. "We can hold all 215 kids from Garrett."

"If no one objects to this, we'll take a vote. All those in favor of temporarily relocating classes to The First Church of Christ say 'aye'."

Everyone on the board agreed to this. No one said "nay".

"Okay, that solves our first problem." Mr. Holmes looked at Uncle Jack. "Jackson, maybe you ought to explain the railroad's offer."

"Wait." Timmy Gilbert's mother stood up, flinging the peach purse over her shoulder. I was beginning to really hate women with big purses.

"Ah," Mr. Holmes said, "I'd almost forgotten."

"I want to know what we're going to do about her, and the fact that she took our children to a bar." She pointed at Miss Mason.

Miss Mason cringed. Vince took a step forward, and Eddie grabbed his arm.

"I've spoken to everyone involved: Miss Mason, the principal. Naturally, Esther, you understand that no one expected the train to crash right into the school."

Everyone chuckled.

"We really just didn't have an evacuation plan for this kind of thing. You have my word that after all this excitement dies down we definitely will be working on one. However, it's November. The kids didn't have coats. We filled every available space in town. The Sapphire Bar was a practical solution. It was safe and right across the street from the school."

"Safe. The Sapphire Bar is not safe."

"I meant safer than the street."

"She had them dancing."

"Well, I believe Miss Mason was just trying to keep the children occupied…" Mr. Holmes was sweating.

"My Timmy is not permitted to dance."

Mr. Holmes looked helplessly toward Uncle Jack.

Uncle Jack spoke. "Now Mrs. Gilbert, I'm not going to speak for your church. That's Reverend Cox's job. I'm just going to say that Timmy, the other students, and Miss Mason were in a tight spot that day. No one acted entirely in character. Some mistakes were made, but I know as a Christian that any mistakes made that day will be forgiven. And as Christians, we should do our best to forgive others."

Mrs. Gilbert sat down in a huff.

"Now Esther, I've been thinking. And I believe that you would be the perfect person to help the school come up with a better evaluation plan. I've seen your work on the PTA."

Mrs. Gilbert smiled and smoothed her skirt with her hand. I realized that Uncle Jack was charming her. Grandma called it seduction. "All good preachers have the power of seduction," she said. I wasn't sure what seduction meant, but I know it had something to do with the way Uncle Jack was getting Mrs. Gilbert to calm down.

"I suppose I could help," Mrs. Gilbert said.

"Great, talk to me afterward, and we'll get a plan of action started so this kind of unfortunate thing doesn't happen again. Is that agreeable?"

Mrs. Gilbert nodded.

Mr. Holmes smiled; he was clearly glad that Uncle Jack had handled that situation. "Well, now that is settled, Jackson, why don't you explain the railroad's offer." Mr. Holmes seemed tired. He took a handkerchief out of his pocket and wiped his forehead.

Uncle Jack nodded. "We've received an offer from the railroad."

There was more mumbling.

"I bet we did."

"I can't wait to hear this one."

Eddie Clayton sat down next to me.

"Now, listen here for a second," Uncle Jack said. "Listen to the offer before you jump to any conclusions."

Everyone quieted down.

"The railroad agrees to clean up the mess, pay for the repairs, and give an additional fifty thousand to the school."

Eddie Clayton leaned forward in his chair, and Vince moved forward and sat in an empty chair next to Miss Mason. She smiled shyly at him.

"What do we got to do for the railroad?" Someone from the back row shouted.

"Now, Lefty, I haven't finished," Uncle Jack said with a smile.

Lefty was a tall, thin man who had a long beard and wore a railroad conductor's hat.

"In addition, the family of each child at Pinewood will receive five thousand dollars per child."

Everyone seemed shocked and started talking.

"Five thousand."

"I could use five thousand dollars."

"Something ain't right about it."

"Now," Uncle Jack held up his hand. "Calm down now. Let me finish then we can argue it out."

Everyone got quiet again.

"It's an all or nothing deal. Every parent agrees, or we get nothing."

"You won't get everyone to agree," someone shouted.

Uncle Jack held up his hand. Silence. Uncle Jack stood up. He buttoned his jacket and tucked in his blue tie.

"I talked to the school district's lawyer. I talked to some lawyers over in Johnstown. I even called Paul Black. You remember Paul. He lived out on Route Thirty, skinny kid with big teeth. He had the beautiful sister, Becky. I know some of you fellows remember Becky."

There were some smiles and nods.

"Anyhow, Paul's a lawyer down in Mobile. I called him. He says it's a good deal, and frankly, our alternative isn't good. We fight it, and we spend months, maybe years in court. Meanwhile, our kids are shipped over to Meyersdale. That's a twenty- minute bus ride. I got two nieces. I don't want them riding on a bus for forty minutes a day. That's just too much. And you know once they're over in Meyersdale school they ain't ever coming back."

There were some "yeahs" and "rights" from the audience.

"Now, the school district could use an extra fifty thousand dollars, and there isn't a soul in this room who couldn't use an extra three thousand dollars."

"You said five thousand."

"Yeah, I did. Three thousand dollars now. Two thousand in trust till your child turns eighteen."

This didn't go over well, and people were angry. Lefty stood up.

"How come we can't have it all right now?"

"Whoa, hold on people," Uncle Jack said. "Now, don't you think it's fair to think of your children's future? How many of you could have used a couple thousand to start off life? I know I could have."

Uncle Jack pointed to a man and woman in the second row. "Remember, Sam, when you and Lucy were first married, you had to live in that small apartment over the feed store with your two babies."

Sam and Lucy smiled.

"Couldn't you have used a bigger place?"

"Hell yeah," Sam said. "We could have fixed up my Grandpa's old place with that."

"Right. Don't you think it could help your kids? Heck, some of them might even go to college. They could use that money."

Some people shouted "yeah". Mrs. Gardner leaned over and spoke to Mrs. White. "I agree," she whispered.

"I know every one of you could use an extra three thousand dollars, times being what they are."

"That three thousand dollars per child?" someone asked.

"It is. You got three kids; you're getting nine thousand." Uncle Jack smiled at Lefty. "You got six or seven kids in that school?"

Lefty smiled. "Counting the twins, I got seven."

"You are a rich man, Lefty. We know who'll be treating over at the Sapphire."

Everyone laughed.

Uncle Jack walked over to the table and picked up a thick folder. "This has the names and addresses of every parent or guardian in Garrett school. I'd like everyone here to sign it. Everyone or no one, remember that. I only need one signature per child. My niece, Helen." Uncle Jack pointed to me. "You all know Helen, Samson and Louise's little girl."

I was embarrassed, and I could feel my cheeks getting hot. Some people seemed surprised that Louise was mentioned as my mother.

"Looks like Samson," Mrs. White whispered.

"Yeah, but she's got Louise's dark eyes. Gypsy eyes, my mother called them," Mrs. Gardner said.

"Well, after this meeting, Helen and I are going to drive to everyone's house who isn't here to sign and get those signatures."

Some people clapped.

"What's the hurry?" Lefty asked.

Uncle Jack smiled. "Lefty, the sooner we get the signatures, the faster the school gets rebuilt, the faster you get your money."

"I just don't know, Jackson. It seems to me the railroad is rushing us."

"You're right. The railroad men up here are sweating. They got a wrecked train scattered everywhere; no other trains can get through. They're losing money, and they're sweating over us, and you know it."

This seemed to make some people happy.

"But that don't mean it ain't a good deal just the same. Is Teddy King here?"

Everyone looked around. Teddy wasn't there.

"Remember when Teddy got his hand cut off at the sawmill? He was in court for years trying to get his money, and he had a clear case of negligence against the company that made that saw. We ain't got no negligence here. The railroad didn't do anything wrong. You think they wrecked that train on purpose?"

Everyone laughed.

"Well, we know Eddie Clayton thinks that," someone shouted.

Everyone laughed again. I didn't understand what was so funny.

Eddie said nothing.

"Listen, I've lived in this county all my life, too." Uncle Jack sat on the end of the purple table. "I seen what the mine companies and the government done to us over and over, and I'd like to be the one to say we could finally beat one of 'em. But the truth, well, you know the truth."

Everyone nodded, even Lefty.

Uncle Jack walked to his seat. "I'm going to give the meeting back to Mr. Holmes." He patted the stack of papers. "Come on up after the meeting and sign these papers."

While Mr. Holmes was ending the meeting, Uncle Jack motioned for me to come forward. I walked around the table, careful not to block Mr. Holmes.

"I'll need you to mark off some names," Uncle Jack whispered. He handed me a pen, and I sat next to him.

When the meeting was over, everyone rushed forward to sign the papers. Uncle Jack shook hands and talked to people.

"I'll sign that paper, Jackson. I got four kids in that school."

I marked off the names of Peter Taylor's children: Hannah, Jacob, Carl, and Max.

"How you doing, Reverend Cooper?" This was Mrs. Gardner. She signed her name with small tight loops and dark scratches.

I marked off her grandson's name, Jeff Gardner.

Timmy Gilbert's mother thanked Uncle Jack for letting her help with the evacuation plan, and they arranged a meeting. Uncle Jack wrote her name down in a little black date book he had in his coat pocket.

Lefty signed the paper and shook Uncle Jack's hand.

I marked off the names of his seven kids. Belinda was in my grade.

The crowd got smaller. Uncle Jack and I stood up.

"Listen, Helen, you get Eddie and Vince to help you figure out how many more kids and parents we need to find. I'm going to talk to the railroad men and help Reverend Paine to his car." Uncle Jack looked around the room. Vince stood talking to Miss Mason. "Well, maybe just ask Eddie for help."

We smiled at each other.

I walked over to Eddie. "My uncle Jack says we have to figure out how many more kids and parents we need to find."

He took the list from my hand. He flipped through it. He wrote 42 on the paper and handed it back to me. He figured this out all in his head. He didn't even need a pencil or paper or a calculator.

"I marked them off with a star next to their names," he said. This was the first time Eddie had ever talked to me. It was the first time I had heard him say anything. His voice was scratchy like he'd stopped talking for a long time and then started again. Eddie's voice was deep like someone whispering inside a cave. I was shocked and fascinated by it.

"Fourteen parents need to sign not counting your grandpa," he paused, but I wanted him to keep talking. Eddie pointed to a name on the paper, and I looked at it. There was a problem. Grandpa was not listed as our legal guardian. It was Grandma's name, Ruby Cooper. She had even signed the paper in her pretty handwriting with all the loops and curves.

Suddenly, I knew why she'd come to get me at the Sapphire Bar. It wasn't because she was concerned about me. She'd even said, "I'm Helen's legal guardian." She knew what would happen and was already scheming to get her share or all of it.

I was furious.

"Keep your cool, Helen. Jack will figure it out," Eddie said and then whispered, "And I got your back, too."

I smiled. For some reason, I believed him as much as I had believed Vince that day on the front porch. They would look out for my family, even if it cost them.

Eddie and I went outside to get Uncle Jack.

"Great," Uncle Jack said when he saw Grandma's name. "How can this be? Dad must not have changed it at the school. Legally, I got to go by the name on this paper." He ran his hand over his blue tie. "Well, get in the truck." He opened the door for me, and I got in.

"You coming, Eddie?" I asked.

"Nah, got to go get Fizzy, but I'll be at your dad's tonight. I can't wait to hear how you handle this one." Eddie grinned.

"Shut the door, Helen," Uncle Jack said to me. I reached for the handle.

"I got it," Eddie said, holding the door. I waited for him to shut it, but he hesitated.

"Go on, shut the door, Eddie," Uncle Jack said. "I got this one. I'll see you at Dad's."

Eddie shut the door, and we drove away.

We bought Cokes and drove to the houses of the families that were left on the list. Most of the people had already heard about the deal and signed without asking too many questions. At one point, Uncle Jack and I led a parade of trucks and cars as some people from the meeting followed us honking their horns.

"Crazy," Uncle Jack muttered as we pulled in front of another house, but he was grinning.

The last name on the list was Grandma's. I knew Uncle Jack had done this on purpose. The sun was setting as we pulled in front of her trailer. The mailbox leaned to one side. It looked like someone had backed into it then tried to fix it by tying it to a wooden stake with a piece of barbed wire, but it hadn't worked.

Grandma came out onto the front porch with a cigarette dangling from her lips. She wore an ugly green bathrobe. She walked slowly off the porch. The sky was a soft color of pink as the sun started to set over the trailer. I watched as smoke escaped from Grandma's cigarette and disappeared into the cold air. Through the small trailer window, I saw Billy Jacobs sitting in Grandma's gold chair.

Uncle Jack sighed, smoothed his tie, and rolled down his window.

"Hello, Jackson," Grandma said. She leaned against the truck.

"Hello, Mother. Have you heard about the railroad's offer?"

"I heard."

"You going to sign the paper?" Uncle Jack asked.

Uncle Jack seemed to be waiting for something. She did not respond.

"Why wouldn't you sign?" Uncle Jack asked.

"Oh, lots of reasons. I could get my own lawyer. I've known a few in my time."

She said the word "known" louder.

"It would be a great way to get even with the people in this town." Grandma smiled.

"What people do you want to get even with, Mother?" Uncle Jack asked.

She laughed. "Oh, honey, I got a list."

Uncle Jack smoothed his tie again.

Grandma leaned in closer. Her red lipstick was smeared, and her eyes were watery. Her hair was flat on one side, and she smelled like The Sapphire Bar. She was clearly drunk and angry.

Uncle Jack looked at her. "You've been drinking." All the seduction seemed to be gone from Uncle Jack. He had no power over her, and he seemed like a defeated child.

"I haven't forgotten what he did to Harrison."

"I haven't forgotten anything either, but I've forgiven a lot."

Grandma blew smoke through her nose. "Not all of us are that noble, Jackson."

Uncle Jack nodded. "So, it's Samson you want to get even with?"

There was silence as they stared at each other.

"Jesus, you're a fuckin' nut," Uncle Jack put his head down and muttered. All the preacher was gone from Uncle Jack, and suddenly, he looked a lot like my dad. "You don't give a shit about Harrison or his memory. Or Samson for that matter. You're just pissed off and bitter."

Grandma opened her mouth to say something. I saw her cigarette drop to the ground.

Uncle Jack was mad now, madder than I'd ever seen him, even more mad than he was at my dad when he first came back from prison. "Let me share something with you. The sheriff did the world a favor by killing Harrison. He was my brother, and I loved him. I loved him when we were boys. But I sure the hell didn't like him as a man. He was mean, and nothing good was ever going to come of him."

"You don't know that. Everyone can be redeemed," she said almost pleading, and then there was a pause, and her face turned ugly again. "Isn't that what your Bible says? Isn't that what your church preaches, forgiveness? Isn't that what you just said about Sonny? He can be forgiven. Why him and not Harrison? Why him and not Harrison?" These last two questions came out of her mouth like wail, and I wondered who she thought needed forgiveness the most: Harrison, my dad, or her. I wondered if she was wailing like this because she couldn't understand why my dad was alive and not Uncle Harrison. Why was he the one that died?

Uncle Jack started the truck. "I'll come and see you when you're sober. I'm sure you won't turn down the money then."

Grandma backed away from the truck. "Get the hell out of here, you goddamn queer," she shouted. Uncle Jack turned the headlights on. He put the truck in reverse and started backing up.

Billy Jacobs opened the trailer door and stepped out onto the front porch in a pair of jeans. He wasn't wearing a shirt or any shoes. There was a beer can in his hand. "Why didn't you just sign the paper?" I heard him say.

"Mind your own damn business," she shrieked at him.

Billy looked at me and something in his facial expression told me he had something to say to me. I nodded. I'll sneak over as soon as I can, I thought.

Uncle Jack rolled up his window, and we drove away. Uncle Jack didn't say anything for the first few miles. He lit a cigarette, but he didn't seem to be smoking it. I felt very tired and leaned my head against the car window.

"This is so messed up," he muttered.

I had to agree with that. I felt small and lost in the darkness of the truck.

Uncle Jack tossed the cigarette out the window. Suddenly, he seemed to remember I was in the truck or maybe he realized that I hadn't said anything.

"I can't image what you must think of all of us, fighting like this over shit that happened years ago. You must think we're a bunch of fools. Maybe you're right. Maybe we're all idiots. But I want you to know that Harrison wasn't always like that. When he was younger…"

I just wanted him to shut up.

"He used to follow your dad around. He wanted to be just like him, but he just never felt like he measured up to your dad. Your dad never expected that. Harrison put all that on himself."

"It doesn't matter now. Does it?" I said, still wishing he'd shut up.

"Of course, it matters. It matters what you think about us, about Harrison. It matters what you think of your dad."

A possum ran across the road; its eyes shone in the dark.

"You didn't always like my dad," I said, leaning forward. The possum disappeared into the bushes.

"I was scared of your dad."

"You think he was going to hurt you?"

"No, not that kind of scared." Uncle Jack sighed. He seemed to be thinking about something. "After Harrison died and your dad was in prison, I was alone for the first time in my life, and that was scary. For you, it would be like losing Joan. Plus, I suffered a lot because of everyone knowing what I was."

I didn't want to think about losing Joan because it made my stomach hurt. I didn't even want to think about what had happened to Uncle Jack, but I had to ask. "What did they do to you?"

"At first, it was just whispering and rude shouts in the street. Everyone avoided looking me in the eye. And then one night, a couple of guys beat me up pretty bad. I was able to get away, by the grace of God. I'm not sure how far it would have gone or what could have happened to me."

Everything got silent, and Uncle Jack seemed to be working up the courage to say something. I waited in the dark silence of the truck. My head hurt, and I rested it against the dashboard. The truck hit a bump, and my head bounced a little. Uncle Jack lit another cigarette.

"I drove myself to the hospital. They nearly killed me, but some of the ladies from church showed up at my hospital bed, and I thought they'd shame me, but they didn't. We just never talked about it, and I turned to the church.

But I also turned away from everything else, everyone one else."

I knew he meant Alex Coolie.

"I thought if I pretended it didn't exist or I didn't acknowledge it, it would just go away, and then your dad came back, and I had to face it. I see things in a different way now."

"What way?"

"Oh, it's kind of hard to explain. I was scared all the time. I'm not scared like that anymore. I accepted things about people, about myself, now."

"I thought you didn't want to be gay. You said that it was a sin."

"I was afraid. I was being self-righteous out of fear."

I was thinking about this as we drove down the road to my house. All the trees were covered with frost.

Uncle Jack parked the truck in the yard.

"I just want you to understand. That's all."

"Understand what?" I asked.

Uncle Jack shut off the engine. "People make mistakes." He said it in his preacher's voice, and I felt a little better because I knew he wasn't mad anymore.

"I understand," I said, but it was a lie. I didn't understand, not even a little bit. I didn't understand how adults couldn't figure out their own lives or why they felt the need to tell kids everything. I got out of the truck, slamming the door behind me as I went inside.

CHAPTER 21

It was Sunday morning, and everyone had gone to church except me. I had pretended that I had a stomachache, and Grandpa agreed to leave me alone for a couple of hours. It was the first time I had ever been left alone at home before.

"Stay out of trouble," Grandpa warned me.

After they left, I got dressed. I had plans to walk down to my grandma's house; I was going to find out what Billy Jacobs wanted to tell me.

Everyone in my house was upset. Everyone had been so excited about getting the money from the railroad. We all wanted a telephone and even a color TV.

Now, we knew Grandma was likely to get most or all of the money. Last night, I heard my dad, Uncle Jack, and Grandpa talking.

"I'm sure I can convince her to at least share some of the money," Uncle Jack said. "She'll sign because she wants the money, and she doesn't want the whole town pissed at her."

My dad made a grunting sound. "She doesn't give a fuck who she pisses off."

"And I ain't never known her to share anything but what's between her legs," Grandpa said.

No one suggested that he talk to Grandma. Even I knew he'd give her everything.

I made my way down the railroad tracks and stopped in front of my grandmother's trailer. I was shocked. Billy Jacobs was packing things into his Jeep.

I approached him, startling him.

"What's going on?" I asked. "You and Grandma leaving town?"

"I ain't going nowhere with her," he said.

I was really surprised. I never thought Billy would leave her, no matter what she did.

He smiled, a sad smile. "Surprised?"

I nodded.

"Me too. I'm just tired," he said.

"Tired of what?" I asked.

"Everything," he said. "The way she treats me, the way she treats other people. It ain't right."

I didn't say anything.

He laughed. "I know you're thinking I should've figured that out a long time ago, but she's good at manipulating people, always has been, always will be."

"Is this what you were trying to tell me yesterday?"

"What makes you think I wanted to tell you something?"

"I saw the look on your face yesterday; you've got something to say."

We stared at each other.

He leaned against the front of his Jeep. "I loved her."

I must have looked doubtful.

"Really I did."

"Why?"

"She was the first person that ever really noticed me." He walked back to the trailer. "I got to get the rest of my stuff before she comes back."

I followed him to the door, but I wasn't going in. Lately, I was learning how dangerous adults could be.

I noticed whiskey bottles everywhere. "Most nights, she's too drunk to get off the couch."

He kicked the bottles on the floor. I watched the brown liquid spill onto the floor and splash on the gold chair.

I helped him load the last of his things into his Jeep.

He sighed. "It's probably not my place to say anything."

Here it comes, I thought, another adult who couldn't figure out his own life and was about to tell me everything I didn't need or want to know.

"She was the one who shot up Alex Coolie's place and tried to hurt your family."

I had been so sure it was the sheriff that it never occurred to me that anyone else, especially my grandma, could do it. "She even own a gun?" I asked.

"Yeah, she does. She threatened to shoot me more than a few times."

What kind of a life did Billy have? I wondered.

"There's a lot of hate brewing in that woman, and she's mean as a rattlesnake. That night, she was angry, angrier than I ever seen her, ranting and raving about your dad. She made me get into the Jeep. We drove to Harvey Foster's. He was drunk as shit, lying in his own piss in his front yard. She screamed at him, told him where Amy was, told him to go and get her, told him to kill Sonny. But the sheriff was too piss drunk. I doubt he even remembered the conversation."

I bet he did, I thought, that liar.

"So, you drove her to Alex's?" I rubbed my arm where the scar was.

He looked embarrassed. "Yes, I did. I didn't know she had the gun until she pulled it out and started shooting. She's a bad shot, and she was really drunk."

Thank God, I thought, or we might all be dead.

"Why would she do that? My dad wasn't even there."

"She didn't know that, and she didn't really care. She just wants him to suffer, and killing any of you would make him suffer."

"Why didn't you go to the police?"

"I told you she's a good con artist. She'd have the cops thinking it was me all along. And besides who's going to believe me? I'm a nobody."

We were silent for a moment.

"I should've left then knowing she could set me up, knowing what kind of a person she really is. But I couldn't do it. Now, here's this money that would make a huge difference in your lives, and she wants it for herself." He sort of laughed. "I'm so messed up that I think not giving you the money is worse than trying to kill you."

"Why did you tell me this?" I said. "I could go to the police."

"You won't," he said. "That's not how you Coopers do things." He smiled. "You'll warn your family, and you'll stick together."

I nodded.

"Wait," he said. He went inside and came out with four dozen eggs in his hands. "Grab these." I did. I watched him lock the door. He didn't look back.

He grinned at me. "I bought them today. I was going to do it myself because I'm not going to have to clean up the stink, and it will drive her fucking crazy. But I thought you and I could do it together before I went on my way."

We both ran to climb the tree. He tossed the eggs, watching them bounce off the roof and hit the windows. We laughed loudly. I couldn't remember when I last laughed like that. Was this what growing up was like? Only laughing when you were doing stupid kid stuff?

After we tossed the last eggs, Billy climbed down from the tree. I watched him. He waved as he climbed into his Jeep and drove away.

As I made my way down the tracks back toward my home, I promised myself that I was going to make my grandma pay for what she did to Billy. I rubbed the scar on my arm. And to me. I wasn't going to let her hurt anyone in my family, not even my dad.

CHAPTER 22

I WAS HOME ALONE, MAKING MYSELF A PIECE OF TOAST WHEN I HEARD THE SQUEAK and thump of the front porch swing. I pulled back the yellow curtain that hung in the living room window and saw my grandmother sitting on the swing, swinging back-and-forth, back-and-forth.

It had been three days since Billy left, and I knew Uncle Jack had tried to talk to her, but according to Uncle Jack, she was too drunk and pissed off to be reasonable.

People were furious that she hadn't signed the railroad paper yet. It was only a matter of time before something bad happened. I knew if Joan and me went back to school before she signed the paper, our lives would be hell every day. I could take it, but Joan couldn't.

I wanted to give my grandmother a piece of my mind, but I didn't know how dangerous she was. I thought about her shooting at us, wildly, in the dark. Would she hesitate to shoot me in the daylight? I couldn't take that chance, so I quietly went upstairs into my dad's room and found his gun. I wasn't 100% sure how to use a gun or even if it was loaded, but I figured I could, at least, scare her.

I went downstairs and stepped outside onto the front porch. The gun was in my pocket.

My grandmother glanced at me with her eyes, but her head didn't move.

She wore a big fur coat, and her hair was flat on one side and tangled on the other like she had just woken up. Her mascara was smeared under her eyes.

She smelled like booze, but I couldn't tell if she was drunk or it was just on her clothes.

"What are you doing here?" I said.

I thought about shooting her. But shooting her on Grandpa's front porch would be a mess. My dad would probably go back to jail for that, and although I was mad at him, it didn't mean I wanted him to go back to prison.

"What are you doing here?" I said again.

"He's gone," she said. Her voice was soft and small.

"Who?" I asked.

"Billy."

I didn't say anything.

"I thought maybe he said something to you."

"Why would he say anything to me?" I asked.

"He said he'd talked to you a few times."

We were silent. She was still swinging the swing, and I stood watching her. She reached in her pocket. I reached into mine, putting my hand on the gun. She pulled out a pack of cigarettes and a lighter, and I took my hand out of my pocket.

She tried lighting the cigarette, but her hands shook so much that it took her awhile.

"I know it was you. You tried to kill us when we were at Alex Coolie's."

She was usually pretty good at hiding her facial expressions, just by having that angry look on her face all the time, but this time, her face turned white, and she genuinely look shocked.

"Don't even try to deny it. I know it's true."

"I wasn't trying to kill you," she said.

"Just my dad."

She nodded slowly. "I told you he was dangerous. No one believes me."

"He wasn't even there, and he didn't shoot up a house filled with kids like you did," I said. "Why do you want my dad dead? Are you still so mad about Uncle Harrison that you'd go to jail over it?"

"Yes," she said, flatly and coldly.

"Well, that's just stupid. It ain't going to bring Uncle Harrison back, and even if my dad killed Uncle Harrison, no one's gonna believe that story; they are going to believe the sheriff's story. As far as anyone's concerned, that is the story, and it's over."

She looked at me then. Her eyes were cold blue. "You don't believe the sheriff's story either," she said.

"He lies. Why should I?"

"You think Sonny killed Harrison, too?" she said. She was hopeful.

I forgot myself and sat next to her on the swing. "Things don't add up." I was relieved to be telling someone about my doubts. Everyone else was so glad to have my dad home that they wanted to be loyal to him, wanted him to be something he might not be.

"That's what I've been saying," she said.

I was treading on thin ice here. Grandma wanted an ally, someone to turn against my father. Was I giving it to her? I felt a slight twinge in my arm where my scar was. "But why does it matter? You're the only one holding onto it," I asked.

"I need to know the truth," she said.

"Why? What would change if my dad walked up to you right now and said he killed Uncle Harrison?"

She didn't say anything. She just stared out into the yard, looking guilty.

And then I figured it out. "If my dad's guilty, then you won't be. You can put all the blame on him."

"It's his fault. I'm not guilty of anything." She had her mean face on again, angry with me, angry with my dad.

Suddenly, I felt like I was winning some battle, chipping away at her until she'd crumble, and I wanted her to crumble. "You did something. What was it?"

She dropped her cigarette and stomped it out with her high-heeled shoe. It was too cold to be wearing heels like that, but my grandma didn't seem to care about the cold.

"If you want me to believe you about Sonny, you got to tell me everything that happened."

She looked at me. "Oh, you're wicked like him, sticking the knife in deep enough to draw blood."

She stood up and began pacing back and forth across the porch. She was like a caged animal ready to attack. I should have run, but I sat still and waited. I had begun to know when an adult was about to tell me something I didn't want to know, shouldn't know. My family was becoming experts at revealing the past, and I was learning to be still and listen for the truth behind the lies.

"What do you want me to say? That I was wrong? That I raised them wrong? Well, I did." She hurled the words at me. "Look at me. You see it; don't you? I'm a goddamn, no-good drunk!"

I said nothing. She wanted me to say it was true, so she could get mad and run away, but I refused to say it even though we both knew it was true.

"I used to think it was funny to put booze in their baby bottles. When they got older, I'd give them sips of beer. Jackson hated it, refused it after a while. Sonny played along, but he didn't love it, not like Harrison. Don't you see? I didn't love Harrison the most because he was my golden child. I loved him the most because he was exactly like me, a mean drunk. That's what I created a drinking buddy, who would be mean with me."

There was an ache in the pit of my stomach. Grandma's words were angry, the anger of a wounded animal.

"It was my fault when he was violent, and I deserved it. When I was a kid, my dad would hit me, and I swore no man would ever hit me again, and they hadn't, not until Harrison grew up and became like me."

"He hit you?"

She nodded. "I hid it. I made excuses for the bruises. Drunks fall a lot. Mostly, I stayed drunk, so I never had to face the monster I created. The monster I had become."

She stopped pacing and looked at me. There were tears in her eyes, real tears. "I had no right to complain about getting hit if I was hitting your grandfather every day." She stopped talking and sat down.

I pushed the swing high. I had to think about this. The sheriff said Uncle Harrison hit a woman and my dad seemed to know what he was talking about.

She closed her eyes as we swung in silence.

"My dad knew about it. Didn't he?"

She nodded.

"Do you think Sonny shot Uncle Harrison during a fight about it?"

"It's possible." I knew she felt guilty again because she wouldn't look me in the eye. "We'll never know unless we know what happened on that mountain."

I agreed.

She reached inside her pocket and pulled out a paper. "Give it to your grandfather. I signed it. The money belongs to you and Joan."

I knew without unfolding it that it was the railroad paper.

She stopped the swing, stood up, and stumbled toward her car.

"If I find out the truth and I tell you, do you promise to leave us alone?" I asked.

"Yes," she said. "I just need to know."

She got in her car and drove away.

CHAPTER 23

EDDIE AND I WATCHED A BLACK AND WHITE WESTERN ON THE NEW COLOR TV. HE sat on the couch, and I sat on the floor. Joan was so excited about our new phone. It was black and hung on the wall in the kitchen. She kept running into the kitchen and picking it up to hear the dial tone. Grandpa kept yelling at her to stop as my dad and him looked through the newspaper at advertisements for cars. Everything felt new and bright like the TV.

But I hadn't forgotten that I had to find out what happened on the mountain. It was always buzzing in the back of my brain. I was always trying to fit the pieces together, and then one of the characters in the Western was shot in the chest.

"It went clear through," another character said.

"Well, sew him up and let's get moving."

"Why didn't they take him to the hospital?" Joan said, coming back into the living room.

"They didn't have hospitals in the Old West," I said.

"But they had doctors. Why didn't they take him to a doctor?"

"They probably weren't close to a doctor," I said.

"He's running from the law," Eddie said. "You don't go to a doctor or hospital when you're running from the law. Besides, after Dr. Mudd treated John Wilkes Booth, you ain't going to find many doctors that want to be involved with a fugitive."

"Who's Dr. Mudd?" Joan asked.

"Oh, now you done it, girl," Grandpa said, laughing.

Eddie started a long explanation of the Lincoln Assassination and all his conspiracies about it.

I stopped listening and started thinking about my dad getting shot. If he'd been shot but he was in trouble with the law or would be, he wouldn't go to the hospital or a doctor. Who would he go to? Uncle Jack? No, he'd try and keep Uncle Jack out of trouble like I would with Joan. I looked at Joan. She was listening intently as Eddie talked. I couldn't blame her; Eddie's deep voice was fascinating.

I smiled and remembered what Vince had said, "We'd do anything for your family."

Vince would help my dad. I had to find Vince.

CHAPTER 24

It was warmer in the churchyard of The First Church of Christ than it was in the cold, damp basement where the fifth and sixth grade classrooms were. Some parents brought heaters to try and keep it warm, but nothing worked. It was recess, and I stood under the stained-glass window with the crucified Jesus painted on it, and I noticed the sleeve of my coat was ripped.

"It's like a dungeon down there," Mark Maxwell said as he walked by me, acting like a hunchback.

Mitch walked behind him. Ever since the train wreck and Mitch Maxwell had cried, he was different, quieter. He never had to sit in the corner, and he was polite to Miss Mason. Mark still tried to get him to do stupid, mean stuff, but Mitch wasn't interested, which pissed Mark off, so Mark had found other mean boys to follow him, and Mitch stood against the wall with me. His head rested against the church plaque. "First Church of Christ, 1924" was what it said.

"Hey," he said.

"Hey," I said, barely acknowledging him. I had been plotting for days. The Sapphire Bar was just down the street from the church. I could run there, talk to Vince, and be back before Miss Mason noticed if I could just get away.

I needed a co-conspirator. That would be what Eddie called it. He said you had to find someone who had the same goal as you did or at least needed something from you. I smiled. Mitch Maxwell needed friends. He had bullied so many people that no one liked him, and without his brother, he needed friends.

"Listen, Mitch, I need to run down the street and meet someone. I can't explain it, but I need someone to distract Miss Mason for me."

"Does it have anything to do with your dad? Is it illegal?"

I shook my head. "It's more like detective work."

He smiled. "I'm in. You want me to do it now?"

I nodded, and he saluted and walked toward Miss Mason. I had no idea if he did it for my friendship or simply something to do, but he did it beautifully, pretending to hurt himself, so Miss Mason had to go inside and get the first aid kit.

As soon as she was out of sight, I sprinted toward The Sapphire Bar. I was out of breath and panting by the time I got there. I pushed open the door and walked in. My glasses steamed up, and it took a few minutes for me to catch my breath. The Christmas lights twinkled above the bar. There were about five people sitting around the bar. Two of them were Fizzy and the big guy from the day of the train wreck. I also saw Eddie. He was sitting at the end of the bar. All his curls were shoved under a winter hat. The hat was black with a skull and crossbones on the front of it. He wore a red flannel jacket. He seemed out of place in a bar.

Vince was behind the bar, and I motioned him toward me.

"Like 'em young, Vince," one of the men said.

"Shut up," the big guy said. "That's Sonny's daughter."

Vince walked toward me. "Helen, what are you doing here? What's wrong?"

"I have to talk to you," I whispered. I grabbed him by the sleeve and pulled him toward the darkest corner of the bar under the picture of an elk drinking a beer.

"My dad was shot. Did you sew him up after he was shot?" I blurted it out, and it sounded crazy even to me.

Vince was silent. Because he asked me no questions, I knew he knew exactly what I was talking about.

"You should talk to your dad."

"He won't tell me."

"Maybe there's a reason."

"Just tell me, please."

"Listen, Helen." Vince put his hands on my shoulders. "I can't dig up the past. I can't get involved."

"You said you'd do anything for me," I said.

"I would. You know I would, but things are different now. I got a chance.

Carolyn and I…"

I jerked free. Carolyn was Miss Mason's first name. "Yeah, yeah, I know. Carolyn and you are in love. Bullshit, bullshit, and more bullshit." I started to walk away.

"Listen," Vince said, following me.

"Forget it," I said. "You lied, and now I got to figure things out on my own."

I sounded braver than I felt. How the hell was I going to figure anything out? I was just a kid.

I pushed open the door. The sunlight hurt my eyes. I started walking toward the church. I felt defeated, and I didn't even care if I got in trouble at school.

Someone walked up behind me, and I jumped. It was Eddie.

"You scared me," I said.

"Sorry," he said.

"What do you want?"

Grandpa would be mad that I was being so rude to an adult, but I was sick of adults.

"What did you ask Vince?" he said.

"My dad was shot. Did he sew him up after he was shot?" It sounded more ridiculous the second time I said it. I reminded myself not to watch anymore Westerns with Eddie.

"No, he didn't. He was in jail when your dad was shot."

I stopped walking and looked up at him.

"Come on," he motioned me toward a nearby bench. We sat down. "Your dad was involved in selling stolen car parts, which you know. The paper called it a ring, but it wasn't really. Just a bunch of crazy hillbillies. I was about your age then, so I wasn't involved in that. Besides Harrison and Sonny, I don't know who was, so don't ask me. One night, I'm staying at your grandpa's and your dad comes in bleeding and high. I'm not sure what he was on, but he kept going on and on about things getting dangerous. I calmed him down and fixed his wound; luckily, it went straight through, and I sewed it up."

"How did you know how to do it?"

Eddie shrugged. "I read a lot of books. I wanted to be a doctor."

"Why didn't you become one?"

He laughed. "Kids like me don't become doctors."

"Because you're black," I said.

"That and I'm dirt poor, and I ain't got the right family. Anyway, when Sonny came down from whatever he was on, he said he accidently shot himself, which I didn't believe."

"Was this the day Uncle Harrison got killed?"

"No, it was weeks before."

"I want to know what happened that night! Did my dad kill Uncle Harrison?"

"I don't know. I only know the story that was in the papers."

"You don't honestly think the sheriff, who got shot in the leg, could have arrested my dad after he was shot?"

"Of course not."

"So, he arrested my dad and then got into a gun fight with Uncle Harrison?" Eddie looked doubtful.

I glared at him.

"All right, all right. You're right. I don't believe it," he said. "The only three people who know what happened that night are Harrison, Sonny, and the sheriff, and one of them is dead, and the other two aren't talking." Eddie looked at me. "You don't honestly think your dad killed Harrison. Do you?"

"Yes," I said. I'm not sure when I began to believe it, but I did. I let that sink in. Even though the sun was shining, a few snowflakes flittered down on us.

Eddie looked surprised.

"You don't?" I asked.

"No, Sonny wouldn't do that."

I opened my mouth to protest.

"He just wouldn't."

I knew the conversation was over. "You better get back to school. I'm sure Miss Mason wants you to make a reindeer with one short leg or a cross-eyed snowman." He crossed his eyes, and I laughed.

I started to head back to the school when I saw them. Amy, Rosemary, and Ruth rushing into the five and dime store across the street. Amy wore big sunglasses, and there was a scarf around her neck. Hiding the bruises, I thought.

When I turned back to see if Eddie had seen them, too, he was gone.

CHAPTER 25

IT WAS THANKSGIVING. MY UNCLE ALEX GOT A FREE TURKEY FROM HIS BOSS, AND Grandpa stuffed it. It was a warm day, so the house was very hot. When I walked outside, Joan was riding her bike in the front yard. Chicken was in the basket of her bike, and he didn't look very happy. She wore a blue velvet dress that Grandpa got at a yard sale. There was a purple bow in her hair.

Uncle Jack and my dad stood by Uncle Jack's truck, arguing, and I moved closer to hear them.

"What the hell do you have a gun for?" Uncle Jack whispered.

"I got it after mom lost it at the diner. I thought she was dangerous."

I hadn't told them about Grandma being the one that shot us. I wanted her to keep her end of the deal about leaving us alone.

"It's a violation of your parole," Uncle Jack said.

"I know that. I don't need a lecture. I need to get rid of it."

"Jesus Christ," Uncle Jack said, kicking the truck tire. "The girls could have played with it."

"I know. That's why I want it gone."

"You're not asking me to get rid of it, are you?"

"Who else can I ask?"

Uncle Jack threw up his arms and tried to walk away. My dad grabbed his shoulder to stop him. "Listen, Jack. I can't give it to Vince. He's on probation, too. Who else can I trust?"

"What about Eddie?"

Eddie stepped out onto the porch. Uncle Jack and my dad looked at him. Joan wrecked her bike by the porch, and I went to help her while Chicken made his escape under the porch.

Grandpa called us inside.

My uncle Alex carved the turkey and even said grace. He didn't have the power of seduction the way Uncle Jack did. I looked the word seduction up in the dictionary. It meant the ability to get someone to have sex with you or win you over to do something. I thought this described both Uncle Jack and my dad.

My dad sat beside Eddie. He whispered something in Eddie's ear. After dinner, Uncle Alex cut some pumpkin pie, and Grandpa poured coffee for the adults while Joan searched for the whipped cream.

Eddie and my dad walked outside, and I followed them to the door. They stood by Eddie's truck. I watched as Eddie took the gun and put it in his truck. I felt like my ears were filled with water, and everything suddenly seemed darker.

I sat on the porch swing. I missed the trains, and I wondered when they would run again. Chicken sat on the swing next to me and licked his paws.

I watched my dad and Eddie. What did it mean that he gave the gun to Eddie? He said to protect us and that seemed like a good thing. I was trying to see my dad as a good guy. See him the way I saw him before, the way Joan still saw him, but I couldn't. Grandma's words rang in my ears, and I knew he cheated on my mom. He was also an admitted thief. Nothing in that added up to him being a good guy. Yet, Eddie, Grandpa, and Uncle Jack all seemed to think my dad was good. I saw it in the way they treated him, the way they talked about him. They understood something about him that I couldn't.

I could ask him about the gun. I could ask him if he killed Uncle Harrison because he hit Grandma. I could just right out ask him what really happened, but something about that frightened me. What if it was the truth? What would happen afterward? Would I tell anyone else? Would anyone besides grandma believe me?

The screen door screeched, and Uncle Alex stood in the doorway. I looked at him but not directly, just out of the corner of my eye. He wore a black sweater with gray patches on the sleeves and a gray turtleneck under it. He wasn't wearing any shoes, and his socks were black.

"It's quiet around here without the trains," he said.

I nodded.

"You coming inside for some pie?" he asked.

I nodded and stood up from the swing.

"Looks like a storm's coming in," he said.

I turned around and looked at the sky above Eddie's and my dad's heads. It was filled with dark clouds.

"Looks like it," I said.

That night, there was a big ice storm. I listened as ice hit the side of the house and bounced off the windowpanes. I expected a window to break any minute. Joan was asleep next to me, her face hidden behind her purple monkey. I crawled out of bed and went to the bathroom. The floor was cold under my bare feet. I was thirsty, so I went downstairs. I tried to turn on a light, but none of them worked because the electricity was out. Chicken was asleep on the kitchen floor. My dad was asleep at the kitchen table with his long hair covering his face. From across the table, I watched as his back rose and fell with his breathing. I poured myself a glass of milk and sat watching him. I could just straight out ask him, I thought again.

"What are you doing up?" he said.

I jumped, spilling some milk.

He moved his arm and then lifted his head. There was a red mark on his face where it had rested against the table.

"Why are you sleeping at the kitchen table?" I asked him as I got a towel and cleaned up the milk.

He lit a cigarette. "You know your Grandpa doesn't have one single candle."

"Sure, he does. Under the sink."

My dad rested his cigarette in the ashtray, walked over to the sink, and opened the door. He started taking candles out. There was a purple striped one, a black one that said, "Happy Halloween", and a yellow one that smelled like lemons. My dad set them on a plate and lit them all. The room looked brighter.

"That's better," my dad said, picking up his cigarette.

We sat in the darkness for a while watching the candles make shadows on the walls and listening to the ice.

"You have a good Thanksgiving?" he asked.

"Okay," I said.

More silence. More ice.

"How come you gave the gun to Eddie?" I asked. I couldn't believe I had just said it, and my voice sounded so calm even though I was sure my heart would pound out of my chest.

My dad looked surprised. "You got prison eyes and ears. You don't miss a thing. Do you? You already knew about it. Didn't you?"

I wasn't a good liar, so I just nodded.

He stared at me hard as he crushed his cigarette out in the ashtray.

I waited for his anger, but he didn't get mad.

"Eddie will get rid of it," he said.

"Why don't you want it?"

"It's dangerous. It makes me nervous."

"Nervous about what?" A tree branch slammed into the window. My dad and I jumped, and then he laughed.

"What I'd do," he said, answering my question. I felt a lump in my throat, and I felt really scared. He is a murderer, I thought as one of the candles blew out. He reached to relight it, and I jumped back. He looked at me but said nothing. The room started to smell like lemons from the candle.

"Grandma said you killed Uncle Harrison because he hit her," I said. It came out of my mouth like a challenge, and my hands shook a little.

"That old woman cannot just leave shit alone, can she?" he asked.

He pushed back his chair in anger and went to the refrigerator and got out the pumpkin pie. He sliced a piece for himself. He left the knife standing straight up in the pie while he ate. I took the knife from the pie and placed it on the table.

"Is it true?" I asked.

"I fought with Harrison about it, and you better believe I kicked his ass over it. You don't hit women," he said.

"But did you kill him?" I asked.

He finished his pie and lit a cigarette. We stared at each other.

"I know what you want from me, Helen. You want the entire story about what happened that night on the mountain, but I'm not telling it, not to you or anyone. That's a door I'm not opening."

"Why not?" I was angry. "Why not tell it? If you didn't kill him, if the sheriff really did, why not just tell it? What are you hiding?"

"Go to bed, Helen," he said, his voice was a dangerously quiet warning that the conversation was over.

I stood up. "I'll find out," I said as I stormed out of the room, but even as I said it, I knew I didn't know how. I had a growing fear I'd never know, and I needed to know. I needed to understand him the way everyone else did. I needed him not to be a murderer.

CHAPTER 26

"What's the point of a colored TV if you two are going to just watch black and white movies?" Grandpa had said earlier.

Eddie and I had just shrugged.

Grandpa and Joan were in the kitchen, baking pies.

"It's driving me crazy," Eddie muttered.

I nodded. I knew exactly what he was talking about although we hadn't talked in days. I knew because the same record was playing over and over in my mind, too.

"Harvey Foster wouldn't have the balls to try and arrest the Cooper brothers by himself although he'd certainly want the glory for it."

"So, if he wasn't arresting them, why was he there?"

"I don't know, buying drugs. Maybe buying stolen car parts. He had a souped-up car then. I can't remember what kind. I'll ask Vince."

Eddie took off the hat he was wearing and ran his hand through his hair. "It doesn't make sense. Why kill Harrison?"

"A shootout between Uncle Harrison and the sheriff makes sense," I said.

Eddie looked at me. "But what your dad was doing or did doesn't."

I nodded.

Eddie was a big conspiracy theory guy. This is why the men at the railroad meeting had joked about Eddie believing the railroad deliberately wrecked the train. He liked the idea that the truth was something different than it was. He liked the mystery of it all, but this mystery bothered him.

I looked at Eddie. "Why did you take the gun from my dad?"

Eddie smiled. "Fool was going to shoot himself again."

I laughed, and we went back to watching TV in silence. I'd been trying not to think about Amy and what I saw, but it was hard. I was pissed off that she had abandoned Joan again, and I had made the promise that I was gonna punch her if I ever saw her again. But I saw her, and I hadn't punched her. Seeing her trying to hide the bruises made me realize that getting punched was just a part of her daily routine. She'd just be used to it. That pissed me off. Why did she stay with him? I knew she couldn't go to her mother's house, but Grandpa would help her until she found a place, and couldn't she get a job at the factory where the other women worked?

Maybe it was another grown-up thing I just didn't understand because frankly I was beginning to think I would never understand any grown-up thing. If being grown-up meant you became a liar who hid things from everyone or betrayed and abandoned other people, I was not interested in becoming an adult, but I knew it was going to happen, whether I liked it or not.

I was afraid of the sheriff, so I couldn't even imagine what it was like for Amy, knowing he was going to hit her every day, and he wasn't exactly trying to hide the fact that he hit her either. He was almost proud of it like he could do what he wanted. Did he hit Rosemary and Ruth? My house wasn't the greatest place to live, especially with my dad getting out of prison and acting all sneaky, but I never worried about anybody hitting me. And the only time I truly felt scared was when the sheriff was around, or my grandmother made me think of my dad as a murderer.

Suddenly, I felt fear creep up from my stomach into my throat, and I left the room. I muttered something about needing air, slipped on my tennis shoes, and went outside. Once I was outside, I just started running down the railroad tracks. I ran as fast as I could. I promised myself I would never go to the sheriff's house again, and I would never care about Amy ever again, but I ran all the way to their house with the cold December wind filling my lungs. When I got there, I was out of breath, and everything was eerily quiet. It was a gray day with the threat of snow in the air, and it was close to dark. No one was home.

I suppose I wanted to be the hero like Wonder Woman. I wanted to rush in to save Amy, Rosemary, and Ruth. But I felt stupid, standing there in the cold staring at their house. No one in the country locked their doors, so I walked over and quickly yanked open the door. I was careful to wipe my feet on the mat, so I wouldn't leave any footprints. I walked into the kitchen. I put my hand on the Lazy Susan and spun it around knocking over a set of mushroom salt and pepper shakers, spilling the salt. I quickly picked it up and tossed it over my left shoulder, wanting to avoid bad luck.

I walked through the living room. All the furniture seemed new. Everything was perfectly in its place, and on the dining room wall, there were pictures of their family, smiling. I thought about how Joan should be in those pictures next to her mother, but she never would be.

I climbed the stairs. Rosemary and Ruth's room looked like any other little girl's room with all the things that Joan and I had like Barbie dolls except their stuff was new.

Across the hall from their room was Amy and the sheriff's bedroom. Based on the cop shows I had seen, the best clues were probably in there, but I hesitated. I noticed the bathroom at the end of the hall. On the tank of the toilet, there was an unusually large doll. Everyone had one of those dolls with the crocheted skirt and plastic head. The skirt hid the toilet paper. This one was big and weirdly shaped. I walk past another room with the door closed toward the bathroom. I walked over and lifted the doll; there was no toilet paper. Inside, there was a silver figurine of a woman. I recognized it as a hood ornament from a car, but I couldn't remember what kind of car.

I turned around, and Eddie was standing there. I jumped but managed to stop myself from screaming.

"What are you doing here?" He sounded mad, and Eddie was never mad.

I opened my mouth to say something, but nothing came out.

"Nevermind," he said. "Let's just get out of here."

"What's in this room?" I said, stopping him.

"Let's go," he said.

"If that's Amy and the sheriff's room and the twins share a bedroom, what's in here?"

I tried to open the door, but it was locked. "Damn," I muttered. Why didn't I know how to pick a lock with a hairpin like they did on TV? Then again when would I ever wear a hairpin?

Eddie moved toward me. He took a pocket knife out of his jean pocket and walked over to the lock. He used the knife to unlock the door.

"How do you know how to do that? You have to teach me."

"I picked up things here and there," he said, "And no way am I teaching it to you; you get in enough trouble as it is."

He opened the door. The room was filled with car parts.

Eddie looked at the ornament in my hand. "It was a Cadillac. He had a Cadillac back then."

"So, he was buying stolen car parts from my dad and Uncle Harrison," I said.

"Nope," Eddie said, looking around the room. "He was stealing them."

"What?"

We heard a car coming down the road. "Let's go," Eddie said. He locked the bedroom door and picked me up and carried me out the back door and into the woods. Once we were far enough away from the house, he set me down, and we started walking toward my house

"He was stealing car parts?" I asked.

"Was and is," Eddie said.

"He was working with my dad and Uncle Harrison?"

"Yes," Eddie said.

I could tell Eddie was thinking. I could almost see the thoughts racing through his brain. My brain had stopped. I tried to think of something to say. Once again, the world didn't make sense to me. Eddie walked fast, angrily. It was all I could do to keep up with his long legs as we walked back to my house.

When we walked in, Uncle Jack, Uncle Alex, my dad, grandpa, and Joan were in the kitchen. Uncle Jack was helping grandpa cook dinner. It smelled like chicken.

Eddie and I just stood there staring at them.

"What are you two doing?" my dad said.

Eddie took the winged woman from my hand and dropped her onto the table. It made a very satisfying thud like the moment in the courtroom on TV when the criminal had been caught with the evidence. I couldn't wait to hear my dad's big confession and decide what his punishment would be.

"That's a hood ornament from a Cadillac," Eddie said.

"Yeah, a classic Cadillac," my dad said.

"Where did you get it?" Uncle Jack asked.

"It's a stolen hood ornament. Where do you think we got it?" Eddie said, directing all his rage toward my dad. "You were working with him. Weren't you?"

"Working with whom?" Uncle Jack said.

"Harvey Foster," Eddie said through clenched teeth.

"Helen, where the hell did you get that?" Uncle Jack asked me.

I said nothing.

"We should report him if he has stolen car parts," Uncle Alex said.

Eddie shook his head. "He'll clean that stuff out long before they get there. You were working with him," he said again.

My dad reached for his cigarettes and lit one. I waited for more lies, but he sighed and said "yes".

The room was suddenly very quiet.

"Yes," my dad said again. "Harvey, Harrison, and I were partners. Things were unraveling. Harvey wanted a bigger cut of the profits. Harrison wanted rid of him."

"Rid of him," Uncle Jack said, sitting down.

"Yeah, rid of him. The night Harrison died, Harvey and I were fighting again about ending our partnership. We had fought about it before." He looked at me. "Yes, he even shot me in the chest a few weeks before that night."

Grandpa looked shocked. He sat down. I felt a wave of fear move through me as I waited for the story.

"We were both out of our minds, high on God knows what. The fight between Harvey and me got violent again, and I shot him. It wasn't that the gun went off, and I accidentally shot him. I deliberately shot at him. Good thing for him, he was running, and I was high, or he'd be dead right now."

A train whistle blew. It was the first whistle we had heard since the accident.

"A train," Joan whispered. We waited for the train to come, but it didn't seem to be moving toward us.

"So, Harvey's shot and hiding in the woods. It's getting dark, and I'm coming down from my high and panicking about going to prison. Harrison shows up. He's calm like cold-blooded calm. Just wants to kill him. Just end him to solve our problem. He said it like that 'solve our problem'."

"So, you killed Harrison to stop him from killing Harvey?" Uncle Jack said.

"No, I argued with Harrison, and while we argued, Harvey came out of the woods and tried to shoot me. He didn't mean to kill Harrison. Harvey isn't that ruthless or that good of a shot."

My dad wasn't a murderer. I felt both confused and relieved.

"Don't do that, Helen," he said.

I was confused.

"I see that look on your face like you're relieved I didn't kill Harrison. I'm a coward, same as Harvey. My own brother was dead, and all I could think about was how I didn't want to go to jail for attempted murder, and Harvey didn't want to go to jail for the stolen car parts. My brother wasn't even cold yet, and

I worked out a deal with Harvey that made Harrison look like the attempted murderer, and Harvey looked like the hero cop." My dad looked at his hands. "Shit, I was going to leave and make it look like I wasn't involved at all, but other cops got there before I could go, so we improvised my arrest story." He sort of chuckled. "I ended up going to prison anyway, but by the time I got to the jail, I was sober enough to realize I needed to be both punished and far away from my mess." He looked at me. "How could I tell that story? Better to be the big scary outlaw with the potential to be murderer than the coward I knew I was."

"But you wanted to murder the sheriff," I said.

"That I did. I'm as cold-blooded as Harrison. That is a mirror I don't want to look into."

And there it was, the truth. My dad shot the sheriff, and the sheriff accidently killed Uncle Harrison over some dumb stolen car parts. And they kept it a secret because they were both cowards afraid to go to jail, and even when he went to jail, my dad kept quiet out of shame and to get a shorter sentence. He made his dead brother the bad guy to save himself. And he said he needed to be far away from his mess, and I knew that included my mom, Amy, Joan, and me. My dad wasn't a murderer; he was a coward who had abandoned me.

The passing train shook our house. Eddie picked up the silver woman, and Grandpa put his hand on my dad's shoulder.

CHAPTER 27

I had promised my grandmother that I would tell her the truth about what happened that night if I ever found out. Now, that promise stuck in my gut and made me uncomfortable. It had been days since my dad's confession, and things were quiet at my house. I hadn't seen Eddie since that day, so I didn't know if he was mad or not. By the time the train passed our house, Eddie was in his truck driving away. I didn't know if he was ever coming back.

I wondered if my grandma would even believe me. She'd probably say he was lying again, and I was a fool to believe him, and I had thought about that. What if I wanted so badly for him to be innocent that I couldn't see the truth? My gut told me that it was the truth, not pretty but the truth, and my dad did admit he could have murdered the sheriff. I also worried that my grandmother would go to the police and tell the whole story, and as pissed off and confused as I was, I didn't want that kind of trouble.

I walked down the railroad tracks toward my grandmother's house trying to figure out exactly what I would say to her. When I got there, the door to her trailer was open, and it was a cold day. I slowly walked up to the door. I called for her from the doorway. I called again, and there was no answer. I sighed. Great, I would have to go inside and talk to her, and that was the last thing I wanted to do. I looked around for her car, hoping that the wind had just blown the door open, and she just wasn't even home, but her car was parked by her mailbox. I stepped into the trailer onto some bright yellow carpet, and the smell of alcohol was strong. I didn't know what kind of alcohol, but it smelled like the whole place was covered in it. Bottles of booze were on the coffee table and lying on the floor. The coffee table was covered with dirty dishes.

I called for my grandmother again. I peered into the kitchen; she wasn't in there. I made my way down the hallway. There was nothing but junk in one bedroom, so I knew her bedroom must be at the end of the hall. I hesitated because I felt a sick feeling of dread. I didn't want to go down that hallway. I didn't want to have to tell her what my dad had said. I thought about turning around and running, but I didn't.

I walked to the bedroom door and knocked on it. I called her name again, louder this time, but there was no answer. I turned the doorknob and opened the door. The bedroom was dark except for a small lamp that sat on the night-stand. My grandmother was in bed buried beneath a bright pink blanket. I walked over to her. I was angry that she hadn't answered me. Too drunk to wake up, I thought. I reached out to shake her shoulder. I could feel her icy skin beneath her nightgown.

"Ruby. Ruby," I said. I shook her shoulder again. "Ruby, wake up."

I looked at her face. She wasn't wearing any make-up. Her eyes were closed, and she looked younger. She looked like the pictures I had seen of her when she was young.

"Grandma, Grandma, wake up," I said.

I thought maybe her skin was just cold because the door was open. Maybe she had drunk too much and she couldn't wake up. What should I do? Should I run back down the tracks and get Grandpa? I started looking for a phone. We had a phone now. Somehow, I thought my grandmother would be one of those people that had a pink phone next to her bed, but there wasn't one. I went into the living room and looked around. I finally found an ugly green phone hanging on the kitchen wall. I picked up the phone. I had intended to call Grandpa, but I dialed zero and told the operator who I was, where I was at, and what was going on with my grandmother. She'll be so pissed that I called for help, I thought.

I hung up the phone and went back to the bedroom. I stood there staring at the tiny clock sitting on my grandma's dresser. It took twenty minutes for someone to show up. I looked out through the curtains. It was the sheriff's car. I watched him and Joe, the deputy, get out of the car and come towards the door. Shit, I thought. Why did it have to be him?

I looked at my grandmother. "Great. You die, and he shows up."

I heard the sheriff moving toward the bedroom, calling my grandmother's name. I wanted to protect my grandmother from him. I didn't want him to see her dead. It was none of his business.

An ambulance pulled up. Joe walked into the bedroom first. He shook my grandmother's shoulder, calling her name. He took her pulse and shook his head.

"Dead," the sheriff said, entering the bedroom.

I wanted to punch him.

Joe looked at me. I guess he expected me to be upset. "You should probably call your grandpa," Joe said.

"Or your dad," the sheriff said.

I looked at him. Suddenly, I had this overwhelming rage. This burning wish that my dad had killed him that night. "No way in hell am I calling my dad," I muttered as I walked past him.

I picked up the phone and called Uncle Jack.

The sheriff called for the coroner, and I had to wait for Uncle Jack, but I went outside and climbed the tree, watching them from above.

Uncle Jack didn't sound upset when I told him that Grandma was dead.

He just said, "Oh, I'll be right there."

That was it like he was picking me up from school.

But then again, I kind of understood. Grandma wasn't nice to him.

My mom was already dead, so I couldn't really understand how it felt when your mom died. I wondered how I'd feel if my dad died. Things were not good between us. It wasn't like I was mad at him anymore. It wasn't even like I expected him to be a TV dad anymore. He was never going to be that. He didn't have it in him, and I was way past needing a dad anyway. I had my grandpa. He took care of me and Joan just fine.

I also had Uncle Jack now. I watched as his truck pulled up next to the ambulance. He got out of the truck, and I was about to shout his name when I noticed my dad was with him.

Uncle Jack walked inside the trailer. My dad looked up at me and then followed him inside.

Great, I thought, scrambling down from the tree. My dad was going to get into a fight with the sheriff again. I walked into the trailer. The coroner and the ambulance guys were talking, filling out papers. My dad and Uncle Jack were in the bedroom. My grandmother was on the gurney covered with a sheet.

I walked to the door of the bedroom.

"I'll tell Dad," Jack said.

"He's not going to take it well," my dad said.

"Why was Helen here?" Uncle Jack said.

My dad laughed a weird short laugh. "You know her. She's trying to put the pieces together, trying to solve the mystery."

"Don't you think you telling her," he lowered his voice, "what you told us."

I had no idea where the sheriff was, but I knew the whispering was because of him. "Don't you think that ended it for her?"

My dad shook his head. "Obviously not. Maybe there isn't an end, Jack. Look at Ruby. She died with so much unfinished business."

"You think Helen and you have unfinished business?"

"If you burn a bridge, you can't walk back over it. You have to swim the river." He walked over to the gurney. He put his hand on the sheet that covered my grandma and started to cry. It was not a few tears. It was sobbing like a child cried.

Why was he crying like that? I wondered. He didn't even like Grandma.

He quickly pulled himself together and stopped crying. He wiped his eyes. "Sorry, Jack," he said.

"It's all right." Uncle Jack said, patting his shoulder.

I felt panicked, and I ran out of the trailer. I ran outside and ran right into the sheriff.

"Hey," he said.

I jumped back and then ran down the tracks. I had no idea where I was running to. I wasn't going home. Uncle Jack had to tell Grandpa. I couldn't do that. I just kept running and running, and then I found myself in front of Mr. Coolie's house, just standing on the tracks. I watched Mr. Coolie's cat as he ran behind Mr. Coolie's house. I followed him and found Mr. Coolie sitting in a lawn chair by the river, smoking a cigarette.

"Hey," he said.

"Hey," I said.

"Grab a seat." I moved a lawn chair next to him.

"What are you doing?" I asked.

"You can learn a lot from nature. I come out here to smoke and watch the river."

"My dad says, if you burn a bridge, you can't walk back over it. You have to swim the river."

"That's very true." He looked at me. "I guess your daddy's been swimming against the current a lot but especially since he got out of prison."

"Don't you hate him? Because you know what he did to my mom."

"I was angry about the cheating for sure. But after Lou died…"

The cat jumped on his lap, interrupting him.

"Why did you do it?" I demanded. "Just give me up to my dad and then my grandpa. Why did you let me believe Amy was my mom?" I hadn't even realized that I was angry with Mr. Coolie until I said it.

He puffed on his cigarette. "Do you know what a crosstie is on the railroad tracks?" He waved his hand in the direction of the tracks.

I shook my head.

"It supports the rails, anchors them, a good solid base so the trains can keep going."

I nodded although I had no idea what he was talking about.

"Do you know happens if the crosstie is broken?"

I shook my head.

"The train might derail." He looked at me. "Your grandfather is a crosstie. He, out of everyone connected to Louise, held it together. My family fell apart when your mother died. Your family fell apart when Harrison died. When the smoke cleared, it was your grandfather that held you and your sister. Oh, many times, George and I talked about telling you the truth, but I never wanted to put my grief on you, and I grieve. I always will."

I stared at the river. "Didn't you think I'd ever know the truth?" I asked.

"The truth has a way of coming out every time, and I've spent many hours by this river rehearsing what I'd say to you when it did."

"And?" I asked.

"Kid, I'd like you to believe we're perfect people who never made mistakes. But you're old enough and smart enough to see the truth."

"But I don't see the truth. No one ever tells the truth."

"Listen, Helen, you got every right to be mad," he said, "Every one of us made the decision to abandon you for whatever reasons we had, and I ain't excusing any of us. Because there is no excuse. But we're in your life again: me, your grandma Helen, your uncle Alex, your uncle Jack, and yes, even your dad, but this time, it's up to you; you get to decide what kind of relationship you have or don't have with us. You get to decide if you forgive us."

I stared at the river, and then I looked at him. "You spent hours out here, thinking of a way to explain everything to me, and the best you got is 'we're not perfect, and there is no excuse'."

He nodded.

"That's a lousy explanation."

"It is."

I was very glad I had my Grandpa Cooper.

There was a rustling sound behind us, and I turned and saw Eddie walking toward us.

"What are you doing here?" I asked.

"Visiting Paul," he said. He nodded at Mr. Coolie.

"Why haven't I seen you?" I said.

"Been thinking." He moved a lawn chair next to me. Mr. Coolie passed his cigarette to Eddie. "I was deciding if I still wanted to be friends with your dad."

I looked at Mr. Coolie and then Eddie. "You told him?"

Eddie nodded.

"Everything?"

Eddie nodded again.

"Do you still want to be his friend?" I asked.

"Yes, I do. It will be a different friendship now because he's different. Things are different."

"Only death can prevent you from making amends," Mr. Coolie said.

"My grandma's dead."

They both looked surprised.

"Really?" Eddie said.

"Yeah, I'm waiting here until Uncle Jack tells Grandpa."

"Geez, I'm sorry."

"I found her. She was in her bed. I went there to tell her what my dad said. Now, she won't know the truth. She won't know my dad's not a murderer like we thought he was."

"Trust me," Mr. Coolie said, "There is a thin veil between the living and the dead. Death won't keep your grandmother from knowing everyone's business."

We laughed.

"Grandmother wouldn't have forgiven him," I said to Eddie.

"Nope," Eddie said.

We stared at the river.

CHAPTER 28

WE WERE AT MY GRANDMOTHER'S FUNERAL. GRANDPA BOUGHT ME A BRAND-NEW dress. It was blue. I wanted a black one because Grandma said you should always wear black to a funeral, but Grandpa said I was too young to walk around looking like a widow. Joan's dress was bright pink.

Everyone was looking for Billy Jacobs. No one knew where he went when he left Grandma, and now they wondered if he would come back and say goodbye to her. There were a lot of rumors going around about how my grandmother died. Mark Maxwell shouted them at me in front of the entire sixth grade class. "Your grandma drank herself to death. Bet, she pissed off the wrong people. Your grandma offed herself."

The coroner said it was a heart attack. Of course, I didn't know this when Mark Maxwell was shouting about her death. I was about to walk over and punch him, but lucky for him, Miss Mason stopped him. She seemed really upset about what Mark was saying, but I was not the least bit surprised. Mark was a jerk, and everyone in town thought the worst of my grandma, and they were probably right.

My dad wore a black suit with a white shirt and black tie. Someone had offered to give him a baby blue leisure suit, but my dad was having none of that although Grandpa was currently wearing a mustard yellow, plaid leisure suit.

I didn't expect many people to be at my grandma's funeral, but there were a lot of people there. I recognized some of them as church folks that my grandmother used to know. Others were people from Uncle Jack's church. The people I didn't know I assumed Grandma knew from bars or other places I wouldn't be allowed to go. I suspected that some people were there just to make sure that she was dead.

But Billy Jacobs hadn't shown up. Uncle Jack started the funeral fifteen minutes late because he thought that Billy might be there. Uncle Jack was like that. Even if he didn't care for how Grandma had left his dad, he recognized that Billy Jacobs and Grandma had some kind of connection.

Uncle Jack made me go to the back of the church to look for him and also make sure everyone got one of those little Lord's Prayer cards. When Uncle Jack started talking, I sat down in the last pew.

Uncle Jack didn't have much to say about Grandma, so he was talking about general Jesus and going to heaven stuff. Uncle Jack had the ability to preach in a strong way even when things hurt him personally.

"Hey," Billy Jacobs said as he slid into the pew next to me.

"I didn't think you were coming."

"I debated it, but it's the right thing to do. I got to say goodbye."

He didn't seem upset. He acted like he expected it; this would be how she would die, alone and drunk.

"It was a heart attack. It wasn't the booze," I said.

I didn't know if that would make him feel better. He nodded and stared down at his hands. Uncle Jack was talking about forgiveness.

"Does she look all right?" he asked. "She'd hate it if she looked old."

Uncle Jack said the Lord's prayer, and the funeral was over. Someone noticed that Billy was there, and the whispering started.

I motioned for him to come to the front of the room. No one came up to him to say they were sorry. They just watched and waited to see if there would be a confrontation between the Coopers and him.

He looked down at my grandma. They had dressed her in a weird old lady flowered dress, and her hair was styled like she was ninety. There was no jewelry, no makeup, and no nail polish.

"She should have red lipstick," Billy said. "She loved red lipstick."

I found Miss Mason and asked if she had red lipstick, but she only had pink. One of grandma's friends who I didn't know handed me a tube of red lipstick. I took the lipstick to the coffin. Billy rubbed a little lipstick on his finger and put the lipstick on Grandma's lips.

"She should leave the world with red lipstick," Billy said. He sighed and looked at me. "See you, kid."

He walked out the door. I followed him and watched as he drove away. When I turned around, I saw the sheriff, leaning against the church wall, staring at me. My stomach was filled with fear, but I was also angry that he had the nerve to show up at my grandmother's funeral.

I walked over to him. "What are you doing here?"

"Paying my respects." He had a bottle of Jack Daniels in his hand, and he wasn't wearing his cop uniform. He pointed his finger at me. "You've been a very busy little girl."

"What are you talking about?"

He wagged his finger at me. "You tend to go where you're not welcome. You tend to take things that don't belong to you."

It took me a minute to realize he was talking about the silver lady that Eddie had.

"You got something that belongs to me, and I want it back." He took a drink from the bottle of Jack Daniels. "But chances are you showed it to your daddy, and the two of you started talking about things you ought not to be talking about."

He stepped forward and poked his finger into my collarbone. "You make sure I get it back," he said poking me to emphasize each word.

"I don't have anything that belongs to you."

He reached out, grabbed my arm, and squeezed. "Make sure I get it back, and you keep your mouth shut, or there'll be hell to pay. I don't think you want anything bad to happen to your little sister. Do you?"

I swallowed hard. "Leave Joan alone."

He laughed, and I jerked my arm free from his hand.

"What's going on, Helen?" Eddie said, coming up behind me.

"Your little friend has something that belongs to me, but you probably know about it, too." He took another swig from the bottle. "Thick as thieves," he muttered.

"You would know about thieves," Eddie said.

The sheriff didn't seem surprised by this comment. "I just want it back, and I want you to keep your mouth shut."

"She's got nothing that belongs to you," my dad said, standing next to Eddie.

"Sonny, Sonny, Sonny, nice of you to join the party. Your little bright sunshine here," He flicked my forehead with his finger, "has something that belongs to me, and I'm guessing she's told you, and I'm guessing you started talking. Doesn't matter though," he said with a crooked smile. "Ain't nobody going to believe you Coopers over me for a second and ain't no one believing…" He pointed to Eddie.

"Don't you dare say it," my dad warned.

"A darkie like him."

I expected my dad to grab the sheriff again, but Eddie stepped in his way. "Not here," he whispered to my dad. "Not in front of everyone."

"Sonny, you ever want to finish what we started on that mountain, you let me know."

"This is not the Old West," Eddie said, "We're not gonna have a shootout. For Christ sake, go the fuck home and sleep it off."

I was surprised. This was not the normal Eddie. Eddie usually didn't have much to say. He wasn't a leader, but right now, he was taking charge of a bad situation.

The sheriff stumbled away from the church.

"Everything okay?" Uncle Jack asked when he came out of the church.

"Everything is fine," Eddie said.

My dad walked over to Eddie's truck and climbed into the passenger seat. "Come on, Helen," he said. "Jack, we'll meet you at the cemetery."

I ran and climbed into the middle of the cab of the truck, and Eddie got in the driver's seat. When we were on the road toward the cemetery, I said, "He threatened Joan."

"And he hurt you," my dad said. His teeth were clenched. "We need to end this. He is not wrong when he says we need to finish what we started on the mountain."

"I already said we're not having a showdown with him. That will only land you back in prison," Eddie said.

"If we do something, I can keep it a secret. I can keep a secret just as well as you can," I said to my dad.

He took a cigarette from his pocket and lit it. "Secrets never work; the truth always comes out."

"Doesn't have to," I said. I reached over and opened the glove box; I knew this is where Eddie kept the gun that my dad had given him. My dad slammed the glove box closed. We were silent.

"Are we going to kill him?" I asked.

"What the hell, Helen?" Eddie said.

"You ain't doing nothing," my dad said.

"Joan was right. He won't leave us alone," I said.

"Your dad and I will handle it. You'll just keep right on being a kid," Eddie said.

Is he serious? I thought. I had a gun pointed at my head. My grandmother tried to kill my entire family. I found her dead in her bed. I was way past being a kid.

We arrived at the cemetery; no one else was there yet. We walked over to the empty grave where my grandmother would be buried.

"I can't go to prison again," my dad said. "I just can't."

He walked away. I realized this was who my dad was, the one that walked away. My dad was never going to be the leader of the final Western shootout. Vince had said he looked up to my dad, but that person didn't exist anymore, if he ever existed. I knew he wanted to protect Joan and me. He wanted to do the right thing, but he couldn't. My dad was forever derailed. Like Mr. Coolie said, he was going to be in my life from now on, and we would form some kind of relationship, but he was not my hero.

Neither Eddie nor I said anything as we watched him walk away; we were now co-conspirators. We were in this together.

"I'm a juvenile. He threatened me. I'm not likely to go to jail," I said.

Eddie looked at me. "There's a big difference between talk and actually killing someone."

"You ever kill anyone?"

He shook his head. "I got to think."

The cars from the funeral approached us.

"We'll talk about this later," he said.

I nodded.

CHAPTER 29

I HADN'T SEEN EDDIE FOR DAYS, AND I WAS GETTING NERVOUS AND ANGRY. IT WAS the last day of school before Christmas break, and all the kids were hopped up on sugar and the promise of a good Christmas, thanks to the railroad money.

The sheriff drove by the school a couple of times every day but hadn't stopped, and he hadn't said anything. I knew he was just waiting for the right moment. He was trying to figure out the best way to get the silver lady back and keep his secret.

I was waiting for the bus outside of the church when Eddie pulled up.

"Get in, Helen," he said. He looked at Joan who stood beside me. "Take the bus home, Joan. Tell your grandpa that I'll bring Helen home."

Joan looked confused. She looked at me.

"It's okay, Joan."

She looked unsure, but she walked toward the bus. I waited until she got on the bus, and then I opened the truck door.

Amy was lying on the front seat of the truck, obviously hiding. I was shocked and mad.

"Get in and shut the door," Eddie said.

"What are you doing here?" I said to Amy as I slammed the truck door. Eddie pulled away from the curb. "Where have you been?" I said to Eddie, "I haven't seen you for days."

"I've been busy."

"Doing what?" I look down at Amy. Her face was bruised again.

"Seriously with her?" I said, looking at the two of them.

"For Christ sake," Eddie said, "It's not like that. She is the one with the most access to Harvey."

"You're so stupid," I said, "She's not going to help us. She'll go right back to him."

"I won't," she said. Her voice was small, and she looked small curled up on the seat.

"I don't believe you. Take me home, Eddie. I can handle my own business. I don't need her."

"Calm down, Helen," Eddie said. "It's all clear, Amy. You can sit up."

She did.

Eddie looked at me. "Amy called the cops about the stolen car parts. It turns out they have been investigating Harvey for a long time now. They're planning a raid today."

"And they just told her that," I said, rolling my eyes.

"I agreed to testify. When it's over, my babies and I are out of Garrett forever."

"What about Joan?" I said.

She did not look at me.

"So, he could still come after Joan?" I said angrily.

"He'll be in jail for a long time," Eddie said.

"Yeah right. The other cops will let him slide. He'll get away with it."

"He's not the most popular guy in law enforcement," Eddie said.

"Yeah but they'll protect their own," I said.

We stopped down the street from Amy and the sheriff's house and waited. We could see the house, but no one in or near the house could see us.

"Where's the cops?" I said.

"Give them time," Eddie said.

We waited in silence. Amy was frantically chewing her nails.

"What if it doesn't work?" Amy said, starting to cry. "He's going to kill us all."

"He's not killing anyone," Eddie said.

I rolled my eyes.

And then the sheriff was there, standing by the passenger side window. I jumped, and Amy screamed.

"You cunt," the sheriff screamed at her.

Amy screamed again.

Eddie jumped out of the truck, ran to the passenger side of the truck, and started fighting with the sheriff.

My grandma used to say, it doesn't matter how small you are if you're crazy. Crazy gives you super strength, she'd said. That seemed to be what the sheriff had because he was beating up Eddie.

I opened the glove box to get the gun, but it was gone. I watched as Eddie fell to the ground. Amy jumped out of driver's side door and disappeared.

The sheriff paused. He wasn't sure if he should run for Amy or go after me. I was frozen.

And then I saw my dad behind the sheriff. He grabbed the sheriff and slammed his head into the truck door. There was a loud thump, and the sheriff grunted, and then there was silence.

Joe Williams, the deputy, stood behind my dad. "Okay, Sonny," he said. "Get these two out of here and find Amy." He bent down and put handcuffs on the sheriff.

"Got it," my dad said, picking up Eddie and putting him in the truck. He started the truck. "Thanks, Joe," my dad said.

Joe smiled. "No problem. Now, I'll be the hero cop who arrested him. I'll be a state cop in no time."

My dad and Joe laughed.

We drove away, finding Amy a few blocks away, running and sobbing. My dad told her that Joe Williams had shown up and arrested Harvey. I knew this was the beginning of the new lie. The lie where we were nowhere near the scene when Harvey was arrested. Oh, Harvey would try and say otherwise, but Joe Williams would weave his tale of heroism, and Harvey would go to jail.

Days later, I took a walk down the railroad tracks. The wind was cold, and my nose was red. I thought about stopping at Old Man Coolie's, but I hadn't decided about our relationship yet.

As I walked back home, I fumbled on one of the wooden crossties. I crouched down to look at it. It was cracked.

I heard someone walking toward me. When I looked up, my dad was there.

"You following me?" I asked. I hadn't decided about my relationship with him either.

"Nope." He looked down. "I read some books about the railroad when I was in prison."

"Do you know happens if the crosstie breaks?" I asked.

He shook his head.

"The train might derail."

I stood up.

"Trains are pretty tough. It would probably take a lot more than a crack to derail one of them," he said.

"Why are you here?"

"Just needed some air," he said.

He walked with me. I waited for some big adult talk, but it didn't seem to be happening.

"You okay?" he asked.

"Yep," I said.

"Okay then," he said, "your uncle Alex wants us to bake Christmas cookies."

I rolled my eyes. It started to snow as we walked inside the house. Eddie was sitting in the living room. His face was still bruised. He nodded at me. I nodded back.

I found Grandpa standing by the stove, frying potatoes and onions.

"If it ain't the river rat from down the tracks," he said grinning at me. There had been a couple of days after Grandma died that Grandpa was sad, but now, he seemed to be okay.

Joan walked into the kitchen. "Uncle Alex wants us to bake Christmas cookies," she said.

"I heard," I said, pretending I wasn't interested although I really was.

A train whistle blew, and I felt the house shake under my feet as a train passed by.

"Do you know anything about crossties?" I asked Grandpa.